AUTUMN ON MAPLE TREE LANE

CP WARD

"Autumn on Maple Tree Lane"
Copyright © CP Ward 2024

The right of CP Ward to be identified as the Author of this Work has been asserted by him in accordance with the Copyright, Designs and Patents Act 1988.

All rights reserved. No part of this publication may be reproduced, stored in a retrieval system, or transmitted, in any form or by any means without the prior written permission of the Author.

This story is a work of fiction and is a product of the Author's imagination. All resemblances to actual locations or to persons living or dead are entirely coincidental.

BY CP WARD

The Delightful Christmas Series

I'm Glad I Found You This Christmas

We'll have a Wonderful Cornish Christmas

Coming Home to Me This Christmas

Christmas at the Marshmallow Cafe

Christmas at Snowflake Lodge

Christmas at Log Fire Cabins

A Stranger Arrives this Christmas

A Train is Late This Christmas

Welcome Home Again This Christmas

The Glorious Summer Series

Summer at Blue Sands Cove

Summer at Tall Trees Lake

Summer at Harbour View House

Summer in Sunset Harbour

The Warm Days of Autumn Series

Autumn in Sycamore Park

Autumn at the Willow River Guesthouse

Autumn in Sunset Harbour

Autumn at the Oak Tree Cafe

Autumn on Maple Tree Lane

For Luna

AUTUMN ON MAPLE TREE LANE

1
MARCHING ORDERS

A book token.

Well, not just a book token. A book token with a coffee-cup stain on it, a circle seemingly perfectly aligned to highlight the expiry date: Sunday, 22nd October.

Yesterday.

Edith Davies pushed an errant strand of tabby-cat brown hair (as her mother called it) behind her ear, and let out a sigh.

She'd dated and broken up with Richard, the manager of the only bookshop for which the token was valid—the unimaginatively titled Richard's Books—so she couldn't go in there anyway, but it was the thought that counted.

So much thought.

The patter of rain on the pavement made Edith step backwards, until she was under the porch overhang of the building she had called work for the last year and a half. She slipped the book token back into the envelope with the word SEVERANCE written in aggressive biro lines on one side, and her surname Davies, almost as an oversight, underneath. She folded over the piece of masking tape that had held it to the glass door and looked around, wondering what to do.

Fifteen minutes after the rain had become too heavy to risk a run for the bus stop—after all, she had expected to be sitting at a reception desk for the next eight hours, and the forecast was much better for the evening—a figure hunched under a wide golfing umbrella approached out of the grey gloom and squeezed in beside her.

'Good morning,' said Roger Westerly, the part-time building caretaker who spent most of his time dealing with Dr. Woodfield's aggressive requests for furniture to be moved or difficult-to-reach areas of the corridor to be dusted and/or repainted.

'Hi, Roger,' Edith said. She nodded at another envelope taped to the glass, then held up her own. 'That one's for you. I think we've both been fired.'

'Oh? Well, thank heavens for that. I was just about ready to do for that woman. You know she was hassling me last week that the cistern in the toilet wasn't aligned properly. Made me get down there behind it with a tape measure. She laughed when I banged me head. No wonder her patients always look so miserable.'

'What did you get?'

He rolled his eyes and held up a piece of paper. 'Twenty percent off a large haddock and chips at Cod You Come Back Later? You know that place on Wellington Road? It closed down six weeks ago.'

Edith gave a little smile. 'I guess she thinks you've … haddock enough.'

Roger rolled his eyes. 'You should make those silly jokes of yours into a career.'

'Well, maybe now I have the chance, since it looks like we're both unemployed. That's … a pain.'

Roger grinned. 'Ah, you're what twenty-one?'

'Twenty-seven.'

'It's all the same at your age. You'll find something else. And I'm getting my pension anyway next year. I was only holding on to see if we'd get a Christmas bonus out of that tight-fisted turkey. You want to get coffee? Pete's van's already open. Come on, I reckon this umbrella is big enough for both of us.'

Pete Markham, ever-cheerful owner of the burger van which came most days to the southern entrance of Brentwell's Sycamore Park, seemed to know more about their predicament than they did.

'Word has it that miserable old mare has jumped the country with a car park developer, avoiding a bit of a scandal involving vandalism of the Oak Leaf Café up there,' he said, handing them coffees, then refusing their offer of money because 'I like to help the unemployed, especially those who need a caffeine hit to deal with the shock.'

Edith sighed as she looked out from beneath the overhang of Pete's van at the sodden park. Dr. Janine Woodfield had never been the most pleasant of people to work for, but with the majority of her time taken up with patients, their interactions had been rare, and the money, until now at least, had been decent. She had always planned to move on, but the last year and a half had drifted past before she knew it.

'I suppose it was the push I needed,' Edith said, huddling against the counter as rain dripping off the overhang threatened to soak her work shoes. 'She was a bit of a nightmare, but you know how it is.'

'Onwards and upwards,' Pete said. 'I saw a sign up in Evans' Carpets yesterday for a delivery driver. You got a van licence?'

Edith shrugged. 'I'm more into pressing buttons. I

suppose I'll have to go up to the job centre. There must be a few places hiring.'

'If I hear of anything, I'll give you a shout,' Pete said. 'Stop by for free coffee anytime. It's free until you can show me your first new payslip.'

Edith smiled. 'Thanks, Pete.'

Coffees in hand, Roger escorted her out of the park to the bus stop. He offered to wait until the bus showed up, but Edith said she would be fine, and waved him off, realising with a lurch of her heart only as the old caretaker reached the end of the street, turned back and lifted a hand, that she might never see him again. Fixtures and fittings, and all that; you never really noticed a light until it went out.

The bus was of course nearly thirty minutes late, and being crowded due to the earlier bus having apparently broken down, Edith was forced to stand at the front next to the luggage racks, bumped and jerked the whole way home. The rain, which had eased during the bus journey, returned with relentless force just as she got off, soaking her as she jogged the last hundred yards to her flat.

At least inside she would be dry, but as she opened the gate and walked up the path to the two-storey red-brick of which she occupied the first floor, she saw shadows moving behind the frosted glass of the front door.

Despite the rain, Edith paused. The downstairs flat had been empty for months, since the last tenant, an unruly fitness instructor called Doreen who'd had a penchant for making a ton of noise and burning her food badly enough to stink out the communal corridor, had been evicted. Marjorie Beaton, the landlady, had often lamented the lack of a new tenant, but Edith had enjoyed the newfound silence after six months of death metal at all hours of the day and night. If this was someone new, she supposed it was only right that she should introduce herself, but after Doreen, she had to admit to a little trepidation. She found herself standing on the front step in the pouring rain, still debating whether to go inside, when the door opened and Marjorie, followed by a young couple with a little girl in tow, stepped outside, thrust purposeful umbrellas up into the sky, and nearly walked right through her.

'Oh, my goodness,' Marjorie exclaimed, patting her heart. 'Edith. I thought you'd be at work, otherwise I might have called.'

'Ah, yeah, something ... came up.'

The couple standing in the doorway looked at each other, then gave Marjorie one of those collective, 'So, who is this?' smiles. The little girl, so blond and delightful she could have stolen porridge or broken rocking chairs, peered out from behind her father's legs.

'Oh, Freddie, Mandy, sorry. This is Edith. She currently lives upstairs.'

The 'currently' was so ominous that Edith's heart fluttered, even as Marjorie covered her with the umbrella and steered her off the path to a communal patio in the middle of the front garden.

'This is a little awkward,' Marjorie said with a nervous chuckle. 'I had planned to call you later. I really wasn't expecting you to come home. I mean, it is a work day—'

'Are they the new downstairs tenants? They seem nice—'

'Well, not exactly ... it's something I needed to talk to you about....'

Huddled under a single umbrella, Freddie, Mandy and Goldilocks were now inspecting a leafless hydrangea as though it were a newly discovered species. Edith resisted the urge to walk away from Marjorie because she'd had enough of being soaked.

'I've been meaning to pop round and sign the lease extension, but I just hadn't got around to it. You know I will—'

Marjorie patted Edith on the arm as though preparing her for bad news. 'Dear, I'd hoped to do this at a better time, but—'

'What?'

'I'm selling the property. Freddie is my nephew. They were renting in Exeter, but their house had a gas leak, and they really needed somewhere at short notice—'

'Well, just rent them the downstairs flat. Or let them live there for free. Job done.'

'But with the little one to think about, they really don't want to be throwing money away on rent. They should be thinking about their futures.'

You haven't minded me throwing away money on rent for the last year and a half. 'But Mrs. Beaton, I was about to sign the lease extension, and you can't just kick me out.'

'I'm not just kicking you out, dear. Without extending the lease, though, I'm fully within my rights to give you a month's notice.'

'But—'

Marjorie closed her eyes as she put up a hand, like a teacher refusing any debate. 'However, the Golds really want to move in right away. I'm happy to waive your last month's rent, which is of course already two weeks late.'

Their surname is Gold, Edith thought. *How appropriate.* To Marjorie, she said, 'It's always two weeks late. I've been paying two weeks in arrears since I moved in. You know I'll pay you.'

'Of course, dear,' Marjorie said. 'But as I was trying to say, it would be much easier for you to find somewhere now, rather than wait until the lead-up to Christmas. You'd then be unpacking while trying to decorate at the same time.'

'Trying to find my porridge mix,' Edith muttered, staring at the floor.

'So, would you be all right to move out this weekend? Or, you know, a little earlier, if possible? What are you doing tomorrow?'

'Nothing,' Edith muttered.

'Oh, there you go, then. I can get Freddie to help you.' Before Edith could say anything else, Marjorie turned to the Golds and gave them an okay sign. 'Good news,' she called. 'Edith's agreed to vacate the upstairs earlier than we planned.'

We planned?

The little girl let out a squeal of delight and jumped up and down. Edith just scowled at her, wondering whether, in the original story, the bears had caught the naughty little girl and fried her up with some olive oil and a little seasoning, until suddenly the child let out a cry of fear and ran back behind her father's legs.

Edith was still dealing with the horror of making an innocent child cry when Majorie patted her on the arm and sighed. 'Thank you so much, dear. I knew you'd cooperate.'

2
HOMEWARD BOUND

'Oh, ah, hi, Dad ... how are you and Mum? I'm sorry to call out of the blue like this, but ... I was wondering if I could come and stay for a few days?'

The pause on the other end of the line seemed to hang in the air for hours. Edith even pulled the phone away from her ear and peered at the screen, wondering if perhaps she'd switched it off by mistake. Then, with a growing rumble like an approaching train, her dad began to laugh.

'Edith! It's you; of course it's you.'

'Unless Ellen's back from America, but I can't see that happening any time soon.'

Edith's dad gave a sudden groan. 'We've already had our invitation for Christmas returned with a big X in the NO box,' he said. 'Your mum gave her an earful over the phone, but apparently she's got some awards ceremony or other coming up that she has to plan for.'

'I ... haven't got my invite yet.'

'Princess, we don't need to send you one, because we know you'll be here.'

Edith grimaced. Dad had a natural way of insulting people while trying to say something nice.

'Well, it's because I love Mum's cooking so much. No awards ceremony could ever compete with a home-cooked turkey.'

Dad chuckled. 'You're right there. No boyfriend yet?'

'Not since the last one.'

'Good, good. We'll have enough chairs then. Mum's lot, Barbara from next door, Stephanie, and you. We're all set.'

'Dad, I've got a bit of a problem. I've just lost my job and my flat. Like, in the last hour. Both of them. Circumstances are a little unprecedented at the moment.' She frowned. 'Ah, Dad? Who's Stephanie? Some friend of Mum's?'

'No, our new lodger. The business has been on a bit of a slide for a while now, so we needed a bit of extra money.'

Edith felt like someone was unzipping her stomach and pulling out her insides. 'But Dad, you don't have room for a lodger. Not unless—'

'She's in your old room. You know we can't touch Ellen's room, but we turned yours into a guest suite. We were planning to Airbnb it, but this way she has to do her own washing. Sorry, princess, your mum's got the TV on. What were you saying?'

'I just lost my job and my flat. I really need somewhere to stay for a few days.'

A loud smacking sound came out of the speaker, sharp enough to make Edith wince.

'Don't worry, princess,' Dad said. 'We can make a bit of room in the cellar. Your mum's been using it a little for her online trading, but we can shift things over to the side. When do you need to move in? We can have it ready by the weekend.'

'Now would be really great. Otherwise I'm under the railway bridge over Willow River tonight.'

'How about Friday? I've got a couple of clients this week, but I'll ask your mother when I see her later if she can move a few crates. Oh, got someone at the door. Give us a call when you're ready to come over.'

He hung up. Edith put the phone down on the table and looked out of the window at Sycamore Park. From the top of the stairs on the second floor of Brentwell Public Library, where she had been sheltering for want of anywhere else to go, it looked remarkably pretty, even in the rain. The towering trees swayed in the wind, showers of yellow and red leaves scattering across the winding paths. Even as she marvelled at the beauty of it, Edith wondered how long it had been since she had felt so desperate.

In the end, Dad called back, telling Edith that they'd managed to clear a bit of space in the cellar. He'd offered to pick her up, but as she stood beneath the bus shelter on North Street, staring out at the incessant rain, she wondered if he would ever appear. Just as she was thinking about finding a dry patch under one of the benches in the park, then picking out some old magazines from a bin to use as blankets, his van appeared around the corner. He beeped the horn as he pulled in, irritating the two other people waiting, then wound down the passenger window and reached across.

'Here, pass on a couple of business cards, would you? When you're stuck at a bus stop in the pouring rain, a bit of wellness coaching can go down a treat.'

'Dad, do I have to...?'

'Yes, come on, princess. My wealth will be yours, one day.'

Edith gingerly offered her father's business card to the other people while her dad made a U-turn in the Sycamore Park entrance. One old woman ignored her completely, while the other glared at her and shook her head. She was pleased to get into her dad's van, even though he scowled as she handed back the cards.

'You've got to be pushier,' he said.

'I'm a secretary, not a saleswoman. Well, I *was* a secretary.'

Her dad looked at her, and the wellness coach persona melted away, revealing the father she remembered from her childhood, the one who had tucked her in at night, made up stories about unicorns and fairies on the spot which were so creative she had resented the onset of sleep.

'Oh dear, tell your dad what happened.'

'I showed up at work to find out that that the woman I've worked for since the beginning of last year has closed her practice overnight. I've since managed to find out that she's gone over to Australia with her boyfriend, and has no plans to come back.'

'Oh, that's too bad. Did you get a decent pay-off?'

'A book token.'

'That's nice. No actual money?'

'I checked my last payslip and it seems I got paid right up to yesterday, but not a day more.'

'What a total scrooge. A good job me and your mum aren't like that. I mean, you might have to chip in for food and bills, but we wouldn't ask you for any actual rent.'

Edith scowled out of the passenger side window. Her parents were good people and loved her dearly, but they were tighter than a supermarket toilet cubicle. She might get away with a couple of weeks before they started to drop obvious hints, but sooner or later, with the reliability of day following night, they would come. It was why she rarely visited, despite living just a few miles away: she was always expected to show up with something. If she was invited over to dinner, that usually meant they'd run out of wine. She'd shown up without a bottle once, and been asked to chip in a fiver, 'since the Tories stopped caring about us working poor, and let bills go through the roof.'

'I don't suppose we could stop at the petrol station shop on the way home?'

Dad smiled. 'Don't worry, your mum's cooking.' He smirked. 'If you could call it that. She's got into all this natural living, nothing out of packets or tins.'

'Perhaps she's worried about your health.'

He looked at her, almost offended, and patted a stomach that had been gradually expanding over the years, despite his line of work.

'I'm a picture of perfect health. If you looked up 'health' in the dictionary, you'd see a picture of me.' He grinned. 'Well, at least one of my company logos. You know, we're planning to relaunch in the new year? No more Rufus Davies: Personal Trainer. We'll be called Internalism: Soulfree.'

As he spoke, he waved a hand, almost steering them into the front of a passing car. As Edith gripped the handle above the door and hung on for dear life, her dad continued with barely a pause.

'With Soulfree, we'll be opening people up to their full potential.'

'Soulfree? Isn't that a bit like "soulless"?'

'No, because it'll be Soulfree.'

'Right. Ah … who's this "we"? Have you taken on some staff?'

Dad sighed. 'Oh, Edith. You're so … closed. I'm

talking about personal expansion here, breaking out of your chains to truly free yourself. For that, you need more than just my help. You need your own.'

'So "we" is you and your client?'

'That's a very insular way to look at it. But I suppose, if you were to stick strictly to the dictionary definition … yes.'

'So, like the dictionary definition of "health"?'

'Exactly.'

Dad clicked his fingers, this time almost knocking over a cyclist as the car swerved. Edith shut her eyes, waiting for an impact, but when none came, she opened them again to see Dad gesticulating wildly, neither hand on the wheel.

'I've got all these new ideas,' he said. 'We're going to take the business to the next level this time for sure.'

'Ah, Dad … the petrol station?'

'Oh, right. Sure.'

Half an hour later, with a free copy of a job newspaper in hand just to remind both herself and her dad that the current situation was temporary, they arrived at Edith's childhood home, a quiet cottage tucked away down a country lane midway between Brentwell and the village of Willow River. Dad pulled the van into the narrow driveway and came to a stop beneath the overhanging sycamore trees along the hedgerow that as a child Edith and Ellen had dared each other to climb. Now, looking up at them as she climbed out, she wondered whether she had just been a daredevil, or if the trees had grown significantly bigger since her childhood, because the thought of climbing them now filled her with dread.

Most likely a bit of both.

Dad went around the back and opened the van

doors. 'Can you give me a hand with some flyers?' he asked, pulling out a large cardboard box and holding it out. 'I ordered these the other day, but I've not had a chance to get them out of the van yet. Since you're here … just put these in the porch, and then come back. I've got three more boxes, and my back isn't what it used to be.'

Edith took the box and walked up the path, the gravel crunching underfoot. To her left was a pretty lawn, bordered by bushy hydrangeas; to her right the pond she had helped Dad build when she was a child. Once clear and filled with goldfish, now it was choked with lilies, and if there were any fish hidden beneath its surface, it was unlikely they ever saw the sun.

The porch was a tiled square beneath a stone overhang. Edith set the box down next to some stone flowerpots then headed back down the path to the van.

'Isn't Mum home?' she asked as she waited for Dad to hand her the next box.

'Yes, she's inside as far as I know. Probably preparing something wonderful for your first dinner back under our roof.'

'But her car's not here.'

Dad gave a sheepish grin. 'Oh, didn't she tell you? We're down to one vehicle now.'

'Really? She loved that Mini. I always suspected she loved it more than she loved us.'

'Don't be silly. It's just the environment and all that. You know, downsizing. Saving the planet and everything. If we all do our bit—'

'But you kept your gas-guzzling Transit?'

'It has more storage capacity. Your mum's car was more for pleasure, really.'

'Like most cars?'

Dad spread his hands. 'Who needs cars when you can have a bicycle?'

'Clearly you and Mum, or you'd have got rid of the van.'

Dad just gave a half shrug as though to suggest the conversation was over. Edith duly took the next box from her health advisor dad with a bad back, and carried it up the path to the porch, just as the door opened.

'Mum, hi, I'm back … oh, sorry.'

The face peering out at her was unfamiliar. A young woman, perhaps similar in age to herself, but it was difficult to tell behind the tinted glasses that took up half of her face, the dark curtains of hair that cut off either side, and the forest green roll-neck jumper that had subsequently been unrolled to cover everything below her bottom lip.

'Do you need me to sign something? Martha's busy in the kitchen.'

The woman had a kind of detached, humming voice, as though it was rarely used. She sounded like a late-night television voice-over, devoid of any emotion.

'Um, hi, I'm Edith. You must be Stephanie?'

'Edith?'

'Yeah, Rufus and Martha are my parents. I used to live here. You might have seen some pictures of me up around the place. I'm Ellen's younger sister.' At the sight of a pair of eyebrows raised just enough to be visible over the glasses, Edith added, 'She's the famous one, the scriptwriter who lives in the USA. She did a couple of Netflix dramas I imagine you've been forced to sit and watch. I'm the family failure, hopping from job to job. I'm currently mid-hop, which is why I'm standing here, holding this box.'

Stephanie didn't answer. Instead, she stepped out onto

the front step, standing up to her full height of well over six feet, and looked past Edith up the path at Dad, who was standing by the van, waiting for Edith to return for another load.

'You have a daughter?' she asked, nudging her sunglasses up just long enough for Edith to catch sight of chestnut-coloured eyes and the brows above them, furrowed in apparent confusion.

3
TROUBLE SETTLING IN

'We're not trying to erase you or anything like that,' Martha Davies said, rotating a wooden spoon through a pot of a brownish lentil and vegetable stew as the edges bubbled, threatening to boil over. 'We haven't thrown any of our pictures away; we've just put them in a drawer. Your father and I felt it would make Stephanie feel more welcome if she thought she was filling a void in our lives.'

'I thought she was just a lodger.'

'Yes, but that's only part of it. She's a little anti-social. We met her parents at a health seminar, and offered to give her somewhere to stay while she worked on opening up her personality a little.'

'So, she's more of a project than a lodger?'

'She's paying rent, of course. Well, her parents are. Stephanie doesn't have a job right now, but your dad's thinking of taking her on as an apprentice.'

'How lovely. If he's offering work, do you think he'd hire me?'

'It would be a trainee thing, you know, less than

minimum wage.' Mum smiled. 'It's basically to get a tax break.'

'How charitable of him.'

'Yes, I know.'

Edith, holding a generic mug because her own favourite Disney mug now had a sticker with STEPHANIE taped to the side, watched her mother as she stirred. Martha was short, rounded, and besides the angle of her nose and the colour of her eyes, looked little like either Edith or Ellen, who'd both inherited Rufus's height.

'Look,' Martha said, 'I know you're probably a bit peeved that we've put her in your room, but you did move out like nine years ago. I mean, we could have kept it as a shrine to you with all your Barbies and Sylvanian Families dolls set up on your shelves like you did when you were nine, but it would have just got dusty.'

'You kept Ellen's room like that,' Edith said, unable to resist a pout.

Martha turned to look at her. She cocked her head and gave Edith a not-this-again smile. 'Oh, darling, you know that's because Ellen's famous. Sooner or later she's going to write a big blockbuster and then we'll be able to charge people a fortune to stay in her room because it's *exactly* the same as it was the day she left to pursue her dreams.'

'You mean, the way it was the day she ran away, provoking a police manhunt?'

'Oh, Edith, you don't need to be so bitter. Having the police looking for you is not something you want to get jealous about.'

Edith sighed. At fourteen, her elder sister had decided that a regular life at Brentwell Secondary wasn't the way for her, had taken her passport and a bag of clothes and done a runner. She had left a note, but Edith, late for school herself, had been too hasty with breakfast and put the cornflakes down on the table instead of back in the cupboard, accidentally covering the note.

That Edith had got in more trouble for that than her sister had for flying solo to JFK—from where she had rung home to say she had arrived, having detailed her intention in the aforementioned hidden note—just about summed up her status within the household. Ellen, of course, had been swiftly forgiven despite maxing out their dad's credit card, her unshakeable desire to become a teenage Hollywood actress applauded, while Edith, who had settled for wanting to do well in her SATs, was met with a nonchalant shrug.

Despite landing a few minor TV roles, acting had not proven to be Ellen's calling, and she had instead turned to screenwriting, becoming, by the age of twenty-five, an award-winning television writer, with credits on several hit dramas already under her belt. Now, at thirty, she was turning her hand to feature films.

And while she didn't always fly home for Christmas—one in every three was her average—she did always call. Edith had forgotten to call once, and that was still brought up as a shameful oversight every year.

'Don't worry, darling, we had cavity wall insulation added to the cellar a couple of years ago. It's nice and snug down there, no more seeping damp. You probably won't even need a duvet.'

Wondering if this was some sideways way of telling Edith she needed to provide her own bedding, Edith just finished the rest of her coffee and glanced around the kitchen for something stronger she might be able to sneak down into the cellar later. Her parents' supposedly healthy lifestyle had never included an abstinence of alcohol, but she could see nothing in evidence. Her mum had always kept a wine rack next to the bread bin on the worktop, but if it still existed, it was now hidden away. She promised herself she would have a search later if the opportunity presented itself.

'Do you want to go and get the table ready?' Martha asked. 'I just need to slice up some additive-free, vegan sourdough and we'll be ready.'

'You're really taking this health stuff seriously, aren't you?'

Martha smiled. 'You're still young enough to neck two bottles of wine, dance until three a.m. and then show up bright-eyed for work at nine, but it'll catch up with you eventually.' She spread her arms, quickly twisting the wooden spoon to catch a stray drip as it headed for the lino. 'Look at me. I creak when I get out of bed. And don't get me started on your father. He's like an old car. He should give himself up for medical research.'

'Do you really think he's going to get his new business off the ground?'

Martha smiled as she returned to stirring the stew. 'If there's anything you ought to know about your father, it's that he doesn't give up easily, even when it's pretty obvious he's getting nowhere. They used to call it bloody-mindedness. No doubt you young people have some new word for it now.'

'I'll let you know if I hear it. I just worry about him sometimes.'

'Tell me about it. But you know, not everyone gets to take home the medals. Think about those who finish fourth, or tenth, or just miss out on qualifying. It's still a decent effort, isn't it?'

'So what you're saying is that it's okay if Dad's new business fails—you know, like all the others—so long as he tries?'

'Something like that. He must have good genetics, though. We raised a winner, after all.'

Edith thought about Ellen's bedroom, eagerly awaiting the sightseeing tours, and suppressed a sigh. 'Yeah, you did,' she said. 'I'll go and lay the table.'

The living room and dining room had once been two separate rooms with a sliding door in between, but Dad had removed the doors years ago in order to make the two conjoined rooms large enough to use as a studio with the furniture moved away. The fact that the floor was fake plastic wood flooring all the way through, with just a couple of rugs to keep your feet warm was another testament to a failed business venture. Now, though, the dining table looked through the space between two angled twin sofas to the television to the right of the window that looked out on the front garden. A bench-like window seat lay along the wall beneath the window, and now Stephanie was sitting on it, her body against the wall but her head framed by the window, so that from the neck up she was a silhouette, like a mannequin watching Edith as she laid the table. She neither spoke nor offered to help, and Edith, feeling a little unnerved, looked up every few seconds, trying to figure out whether or not Stephanie had moved. With her hands laid across her lap, her feet pushed tightly together, she could have been waiting for a job interview. Edith had the urge to shout out 'Next!', just to see if it cajoled Stephanie into some form of action.

Only when Martha appeared with the steaming pot of stew held precariously between two oven-gloved hands, did Stephanie suddenly snap upright as though standing to attention. She towered over the rest of them like a cuckoo in a sparrow's nest. Edith wondered how long it would be before she was pushed out of the nest for good.

'Can you call your father?' Martha said, turning back to the kitchen. Edith opened her mouth to answer, but Stephanie suddenly replied with 'Yes, Mother,' then marched marionette-like out of the room, leaving Edith staring after her, wondering if the underside of the Brentwell railway bridge might be a better option.

A couple of minutes later, Stephanie returned with Rufus trailing behind her. He wore only shorts and a figure-hugging t-shirt now which had an oval of sweat from his neck down to his protruding stomach, as though he'd been exercising.

'Right, let's eat,' Martha said, clapping her hands together.

Edith went to sit down, but Rufus put out a hand. 'First, we must give thanks.'

'Oh?' Edith lifted an eyebrow. This was new.

Martha chuckled. 'Your father's decided to start a religion,' she said, then added in a whisper that was loud enough for everyone to hear, 'Religions don't have to pay taxes, you know.'

'Oh, honey, you're such a sceptic,' Rufus said. 'I'll make a disciple of you yet.'

Martha gave Edith a wink. 'The robes are on order.'

'To Fieldy, Lord of the Harvest, we give thanks for what we are about to consume, and to His grateful servant, Martha Davies, for transforming His fruits into a table of delights.'

'Dad, seriously, "Fieldy"?'

'It's a placeholder,' Martha said. 'Until he thinks of something better. To Fieldy!'

'To Fieldy,' Stephanie mumbled, bowing slightly and then sitting down, as though this was a known nightly routine. Edith muttered the same in order to appease her father, then lowered herself back into her seat, trying to avoid looking at Stephanie, sitting across from her.

'Well, this is nice,' Martha said, her tone requiring everyone, even Stephanie, to look at her. 'Like a proper family. Just the one missing, but did you know Ellen's new show opened at No. 2 in Netflix's weekly ranking? A decent excuse to be absent, don't you think?'

Edith of course did know, having been texted the news by both her mother and father, two of her sister's old schoolfriends, and even been tagged in a post about it on social media.

'Good for her,' she said.

'Congratulations,' Stephanie mumbled, staring straight ahead at a tray of seasonings and sauces in the middle of the table.

'Have you seen any of my sister's shows?' Edith asked.

'Sister?'

As Stephanie shifted uncomfortably, Martha patted Edith on the arm. 'She's still coming to terms with it,' she whispered. 'We told her Ellen was our niece.'

'Right. As you do.'

Edith decided it might be better to adopt Stephanie's approach and get through this most awkward of dinners as quickly as possible. Ducking her head, she began to tuck into a stew that was a lot tastier than its threat of healthiness suggested.

After the stew, her mother served up a kind of tofu yoghurt dish with a sweet sauce, which again tasted better than it deserved to. Edith, who ate far too much packet food out of the Tesco on Brentwell High Street, was at least appreciative of a little home cooking. She wasn't sad, however, when dinner was over, and after a brief and weird moment of thanks once more to Fieldy, they were able to leave the table.

Stephanie immediately shuffled off to her—meaning formerly Edith's—room, while Rufus complained of backache, and Martha informed them all that she needed to make an urgent phone call.

Leaving Edith to wash up, of course.

Standing in the kitchen, looking out at the shadowy back garden lit only by the kitchen strip light behind her, she felt the first sense of peace since coming home. At least she had a roof over her head. Not everything was bad. And it didn't have to be for long—she could go to the job centre in the morning, maybe get something before Christmas, then perhaps start looking for another place to live. The thought of flat-sharing filled her with dread—she'd had one housemate at university who hadn't washed for a year as a kind of science experiment—but it would be preferable to living here. And while rents had skyrocketed since she had got her current place, there were a couple of new-builds near the station offering bedsits at a pretty affordable price. She would finally get to understand how Jeepers—her childhood pet rabbit—had felt, but at least she would have her freedom. Jeepers had chewed his way out and met his demise at the claws of next door's cat, but Edith would at least have a key.

Then, no more awkward dinners, no more Fieldy, no more empty ambitions doomed to failure.

And no more—

A shadow fell on her. Edith's breath caught in her throat. She looked up at the window, and saw a figure looming Michael Myers-like at her shoulder. She struggled to breathe as Stephanie lifted her hands, but instead of a knife, a garotte, or a baseball bat, she held up a tea towel.

'I can dry,' she said.

'Uh ... thanks. I mean, you don't have to; if you leave it long enough it'll pretty much dry itself, but you know, if you're not busy.'

'I'm not busy. I've finished my ... affirmations.'

'Your ... affirmations?'

Edith glanced back over her shoulder. Stephanie was staring out into the night. 'He's back,' she said.

'Who? Uh ... Fieldy?'

Stephanie didn't smile. 'The squirrel. There, on the bird table. A thief in the night. Like ... me.'

Edith wondered why Stephanie hadn't been on Dr. Woodfield's list of patients. She would have been a perfect case study.

'What happened?'

'I stole a man's heart.'

'You did?' Tall and broad-shouldered with a weird sense of fashion, Stephanie didn't look much like a heartbreaker, but as Martha had once told Edith during her school days after someone had bullied her for a perm she had mistakenly thought would make her attractive but had instead turned her into an eighties hair metal groupie, 'there's someone for everyone.'

'His external pacemaker,' Stephanie said. 'I thought it was an iPod. I wanted to sell it. He ended up in hospital.'

Edith nearly coughed. 'Oh. You mean you literally stole a man's heart?'

'And his television. His microwave, his toaster, his sandwich-maker.'

For a moment Edith wondered if Stephanie would break into a dance one of her housemates had done at university whenever they went to a club, mocking the ravers and their hand movements. Microwave, toaster, sandwich-maker....

Instead, Stephanie just stood and stared out of the

window into the garden. 'He'll steal anything,' she said, presumably referring again to the squirrel. 'He doesn't need it, but he steals it, and he hides it away….'

Edith continued to pile washed dishes on the drying tray, but so far, Stephanie was yet to touch anything.

'He doesn't even want it,' Stephanie said in the same, slow monotone, as though she were talking in her sleep. 'He doesn't want it, but he has to have it; he has to take it—'

'Everything all right in here?' came Martha's voice from the door to the hall, making Edith jump, suds from her hands spraying across the window. 'Ah, you're bonding. How nice.'

As she disappeared into the hall, Stephanie said, 'He's gone, vanished, disappeared into thin air. No way to know he was ever there, except for the empty space left behind.'

She put down the tea towel, turned and walked away, out into the hallway, until Edith heard the soft click of her old bedroom door closing.

'As I said,' she said quietly to herself, glancing at the pile of dishes. 'They'll dry themselves.'

4

INTO THE CELLAR

'Mum ... why is there a lock on my bedroom door? Specifically on the outside?'

Martha flapped a hand over her shoulder as Edith followed her out of the utility room, where Martha had just stored a bag of rubbish before tomorrow's collection, back into the kitchen.

'Oh, it's nothing.'

'Is there something you're not telling me about Stephanie? In addition to not telling me about her at all?'

'Nothing you need to worry about. Just that Stephanie informs us when she's about to turn in, and we ... you know, slide the lock.'

'Is she dangerous?'

Martha chuckled. 'Oh, don't be silly. It's more for her than it is for us.'

'What possible reason could she have for needing to be locked in at night?'

Martha put a hand on Edith's arm. 'Shh! Keep your voice down. I don't want her to overhear you talking about her like that. She's extremely sensitive about her … situation.'

'And what situation is that, Mum?'

Martha just sighed. 'Look, I've got to get a load of washing on. Ask your father. He understands it much better than me.'

Edith found Rufus out in the garage, standing in front of a newly installed floor-to-ceiling mirror, practising yoga moves on a tiger print rug while river sounds drifted out of a CD player in the corner. He looked up and smiled as she came in and sat down on the edge of the rug.

'I don't know why you don't just open the garage door,' she said, patting him on the shoulder as he attempted to pull his left foot up to touch his right elbow. 'You'd be able to hear an actual river.'

It wasn't quite true unless it had been raining heavily; Willow River was on the other side of the main road and was generally quite quiet. Rufus just gave her a smile as he untwisted himself, wiped sweat off his brow, and sat up.

'Midges and moths,' he said. 'Your mother would kill me.'

'Put a screen up. Or better still, put a brighter light outside, so they all fly to that instead.'

'Look at you, being all practical. You're wasted on secretarial work.'

'A good job I'm no longer doing it,' she said, staring at herself in the mirror, trying to psyche herself up to what she really wanted to ask. 'Ah … Dad … what's the deal with Stephanie? I saw the lock on the door, and Mum told me to ask you about it.'

Rufus turned to look at her, then frowned. 'You mustn't say anything about it to her,' he said. 'She's very sensitive.'

'That's what Mum said. What's up with her?'

'She's a kleptomaniac.'

'A what?'

'She steals things. Compulsively. She can't help herself. She doesn't do it because she wants what she steals, she just enjoys the feeling it gives her. That's why we lock her up, so that nothing goes missing during the night.'

'And … you thought you'd just offer her a place to stay? What, until you run out of things for her to steal?'

Rufus sighed. 'Don't be so critical, princess. To be honest, we didn't really believe it until I found her burying your grandmother's china teapot at the bottom of the garden. She was so embarrassed when we confronted her about it. She promised not to do it again and the locks went on the doors. Well, specifically Ellen's room and yours. Now we know what she's up to, if we find anything missing, we write it on a list and she brings it back.'

'That's nuts.'

'Don't be unkind. It's a medical condition.'

Edith forced a smile. 'How nice of you to offer charity.'

'I knew you'd understand.'

∼

With Dad in the garage and Mum busying herself in the kitchen, Edith wanted to watch some television, but couldn't find the remote. By the time she discovered it, rather frustratingly on the windowsill behind the closed living room curtain, with a piece of paper emblazoned with the word NO! taped to the back, she was too tired to bother. She informed Martha she was ready for bed.

'Great,' Martha said, rubbing her hands together. 'We've set up the camp bed in the cellar. It's a nice one we got on sale in Wright's the other week, so you won't be completely roughing it. Obviously if you're planning to stay a while, we can think about getting something sturdier.'

'I'm sure it'll be fine.'

'Great. Do you want me to show you down or can you remember?'

Edith nodded. 'I'll be fine. Have you got a decent light down there now?'

Marta smiled. 'Yes, we replaced that creepy swinging thing a while back. You can switch it on from the top of the steps, so no worries about having to go down there and flail around in the dark for the string, while the zombies are reaching out for you.'

Edith grimaced. 'That's a relief.'

'Gosh, I remember how you and your friends used to dare each other to go down there as kids.'

'I remember.'

'Then you tried it as teenagers and that young man Gary fell down and his parents tried to sue us. Do you remember that?'

'How could I forget? I had to stand outside for the ambulance for more than an hour in the freezing cold.'

'You didn't push him, did you?'

'No! He was on the tequila. He got halfway down and tripped on his shoelace.'

'Well, that's a relief. We thought you were lying at the time, but we lied to the police because we didn't want you to have a criminal record at such a young age.'

'Uh … thanks?'

'Once you start on a life of crime, it's hard to turn away. You know, I saw him the other day in the supermarket. Gary. He still walks with a limp.'

'He walked with a limp before. He had one short leg. That's probably why he tripped. The tequila made him think they were both the same length.'

Martha smiled. 'Those were the days. I miss you two girls being teenagers sometimes. Not often, but once in a while. Anyway, your dad's put a carpet on the stairs now so you shouldn't have to worry about slipping. And a banister, but that's mostly because of him and his back.'

'Why doesn't he pray to Fieldy for a little pain relief?'

'Oh, Edith, you can be sharp sometimes.' Then, lowering her voice, Martha said, 'Fieldy only really deals with the food, don't you know?'

Just as Edith was beginning to think her mother was serious, Martha let out a little giggle. 'Right, I'm off to bed too. You should be all right down there. Don't move any of the boxes. I have all my stuff in order.'

'Okay.'

Unsure what her mother meant, Edith got ready for bed, then headed for the cellar stairs to face the door that represented all of her childhood fears.

To be fair to her parents, the cellar looked a lot different to how it had when Edith was a kid. Back then it had been a dank and creepy place, sticky concrete floors and walls, a single hanging bulb overhead with its pull cord, and filled with dusty cardboard boxes overflowing with junk. The fear had come simply from having to get down the stairs to the middle of the room before being able to reach the light cord, but now, as Edith pressed the switch at the top of the stairs to find a green carpeted stairway leading down to a well-lit, pleasant space with carpet, tasteful floral wallpaper and a plastered ceiling, she didn't feel quite so bad. In fact, it was almost nice. So nice, she wondered why they hadn't given it to Stephanie.

Only as she got to the bottom of the stairs did she realise. The space had always opened up as you reached the bottom, stretching back beneath half of the house, but besides the little square visible from above where a camp bed had been set out, the cellar was now stacked high with crates and boxes, most of them covered with old curtains to keep off the dust.

Whatever her mother was buying and selling, there was a lot of it, and it would be looming over Edith while she slept.

Her curiosity getting the better of her, Edith couldn't help but reach out and pull back the nearest curtain.

'Oh!'

She jumped back, dropping the curtain. Heart racing, she reached out and gave it a tentative tug, revealing the corner of the monstrosity she had thought she had seen.

'Mum … what on earth are you doing?'

She tugged back the curtain a little further, a tingle of horror running down her back. Not crates, but glass cabinets, stacked up three high. Rows and rows of them. And in each one, a gruesome scene depicting a number of dusty stuffed animals dressed up and arranged to be in the middle of some kind of activity. Rabbits having a tea party. A group of field mice playing cricket. Half a dozen moles ballroom dancing. The macabre scenes went on and on as Edith looked under one curtain after another. There were more, too: stuffed birds and fish, a glassy-eyed badger standing on a tree stump. A pair of lambs, their wool now threadbare, frolicking for all eternity in a field made of plywood painted green and topped with shredded paper, noses reaching for the dried, crispy remains of a butterfly impaled on an arching piece of copper wire.

Brentwell's railway bridge wasn't just appealing now; it was preferable.

'Are you all right down there?' called Martha from the top of the stairs. 'Would you like a bedside lamp or anything?'

'No, I'm fine,' Edith croaked, gently lowering the curtain back down over the two long-dead lambs.

'Okay, that's great. Well, I can turn the light out from up here so you don't need to come back up the stairs.'

'Mum, wait—'

'Night, dear!' Martha called, and the air escaped Edith's lungs in a sudden horrified gasp as she found herself plunged into darkness. At the top of the stairs the door clicked shut, followed by the thud of a lock turning.

'Mum? Why did you lock the door? There's no need…!' Edith's head slumped forwards onto her chest. Of course there was no need, but her mum had probably done it out of habit, immediately forgetting Edith was even down here. She could scream and holler, create a fuss, but she wasn't just tired, she was weary. Life could be almost painful sometimes. She felt behind her for the camp bed then lay down, squeezing her eyes shut, wishing as she did so that she wouldn't hear the gentle, mocking laughter of a hundred long-dead stuffed animals, clinking their teacups together and tipping their top hats.

5
A POSSIBLE ESCAPE

'You don't look like you slept well, princess,' Rufus said, pouring coffee out of a filter into a cup and then stirring in a little soya milk. 'Coffee? I can stir in a spoonful of dregs if you want something a little stronger.'

Edith rubbed her eyes and pushed a clump of hair out of her face. 'I suppose I'm used to my old bed,' she said. 'Yeah, coffee would be good.'

'Good morning!' Martha said, clapping her hands as she bounced into the kitchen. 'How is everyone this morning? Rufus, have you let Stephanie out yet?'

'Just let me make the coffee, then I'll go and knock, see if she's up,' he said, putting a cup down in front of Edith, who frowned at how the soya milk had curdled, floating around in little clumps like bacteria suspended in a solution. 'You know how she tends to sleep late.'

'You don't look like you slept at all,' Martha said to Edith. 'Were you cold? Do you want me to put a little heater down there tonight? I'm sorry about locking the door.' She rolled her eyes and let out a chirpy laugh. 'With everything down there, I have to keep it locked for security reasons. Make sure you shout if I do it again tonight.'

Tonight. The thought of another night locked in the dark, trying to sleep while surrounded by dead animals, filled Edith with dread. She had woken up around midnight, felt for her phone to check the time, and in the spectral glow found that the nearest curtain had slipped off, and a dozen stuffed voles and weasels had appeared to be watching her sleep. The rest of the night had passed in fitful restlessness with the duvet pulled over her head.

'Okay, Mum, I will.' Edith gave her coffee an overly dramatic stir. 'Mum … what are those things doing down there anyway? Why on earth do you even have them?'

'Oh, you mean those art displays?' She rubbed her chin. 'Those….'

Rufus stood up. 'I'll go and unlock Stephanie's room,' he said, heading for the door.

'Yes, Mum. Those *art displays*. You have half the British countryside down there.'

'It's just a bit of buying and selling. I'm kind of an intermediary for a group of taxidermy enthusiasts.'

Edith rubbed her eyes. 'Why can't you just get a proper job? Like in the supermarket or something? A café? There must be a million things you can do that don't involve having a cellar full of stuffed animals.'

'Oh come on, dear. Can't you use it for one of your comedy routine jokes? Wasn't that how you were going to follow Ellen into the entertainment industry?'

'Oh, Mum, I'm not doing anything like that anymore. How long are they going to be there, anyway?'

Martha shifted from foot to foot. 'That's the thing, isn't it? A couple of the big investors are locked in a bit of a bidding war. I'm kind of in limbo at the moment.'

The kitchen door opened and Stephanie appeared, so

tall she had to duck her head to get inside. She wore a pair of Edith's old slippers, grey pyjama bottoms and a Superman t-shirt, on which someone had added 'tephanie' in small black letters after the initial S.

'Good morning,' she said with a sigh as though it were anything but.

'Coffee?' Edith said, jumping up, thinking perhaps that Stephanie might be the least complicated of the three people she was now living with. 'Did you sleep okay?'

'No,' Stephanie said. 'I had a bad dream.'

'Oh, really?'

'Yes. Something was outside my window, calling me, but I couldn't get out; I couldn't get to it.'

'Perhaps it was Fieldy?' Edith suggested, getting a light smack on her arm from Martha and a roll of the eyes.

'No, Fieldy is an abstract being,' Stephanie said, without any hint of humour. 'He exists only in our beliefs.'

'Perhaps he sent a … disciple? Maybe Alan from next door?'

'Don't be mean,' Martha hissed.

Chastened yet frustrated at the same time, Edith returned to stirring her coffee. Stephanie, seemingly unperturbed, poured one for herself and then headed for the toaster in the corner.

Breakfast passed quietly, Edith eating a bowl of cornflakes while Stephanie crunched her way through four slices of overcooked toast. Martha sat between them, looking from one to the other as though trying to familiarise two pet dogs. Edith, staring out of the window at the bird feeder on which a handful of blue tits were bickering over some sunflower seeds, could think of nothing other than a possible escape route.

After breakfast she announced that she was heading into Brentwell to visit the job centre. She almost considered suggesting that they all go, make a day trip of it, perhaps share a sandwich between the four of them in Sycamore Park afterwards while they discussed possible forms of employment to improve on self-help, stuffed animal trading, theft, and none. However, part of the reason to go was to escape from her dysfunctional family plus one for a few hours, maybe even look for somewhere else to live while she was at it.

She duly caught a bus back into Brentwell and walked up the high street to the job centre. A few places were hiring, but they were almost exclusively part-time seasonal positions ending after Christmas, paying less than minimum wage, with the little caveat 'ideal for students' somewhere on the job description. Afterwards, feeling deflated, Edith walked on to the local letting agency, where her slowly deflating balloon was unceremoniously popped at the sight of the only rental prices available. It didn't take a calculator to tell her that she would need at least two full-time jobs just to afford a deposit on a new place. There were a few house-shares available, but even those were at the very top of her price range, and also contained 'ideal for students' somewhere on the ad, which to Edith meant she would be dealing with all-night parties, uncleaned kitchens, decomposing food left lying around the living room, and toilets so unclean they were practically evolving into life forms capable of consuming humans. She hadn't minded it at twenty-one, but at twenty-seven it filled her with dread, leaving her parents' Cellar of Victorian Horrors as a somewhat preferable option.

After dropping by Sycamore Park to say hello to Pete Markham, she reluctantly caught the bus back home. Stephanie was outside, digging over her parents' vegetable garden, but Martha and Rufus both came to the door to meet her with uncharacteristic enthusiasm.

'How was the job and flat search?' Martha said, rubbing her hands together while Rufus leaned over her shoulder like a hungry dog wanting to get at lunch.

'Not very productive—'

'Oh, that's too bad,' Martha interrupted. 'But don't worry, your dad has some news.'

Rufus grinned. 'It just so happens that I found a solution to your problem,' he said. 'At least in the short term. The long term ... we'll cross that bridge, and all that. But I was out jogging this morning and I ran into Arnold Pickles—'

'You jog, Dad?'

'Every morning, I'll have you know.' He lifted an eyebrow which defied her to question him. Edith just humoured him with a smile.

'Isn't Arnold Pickles the man who owns that haunted old manor house down Maple Tree Lane?'

'Trenton Manor, yes. You remember well, princess. So, I bumped into him—not literally; I can't afford a lawsuit—and he told me something interesting. Very interesting, in fact.'

From his tone, it was clear to Edith that it was more interesting to her dad that it would likely be to her, but she decided to play along. 'Come on, spill the beans. The suspense is literally killing me.'

'I can imagine,' Rufus said, beaming with self-importance. 'Anyway, Mr. Pickles—sorry, *Lord* Pickles—told me that he has a few health problems, and as a result is planning to sell that old hulk he has up the road there, and move abroad. He just popped down from London to see what kind of state it's in. He told me it's a bit mothballed, and needs a bit of a tidy up, a vacuum put round, that kind of thing.'

'I'm sure he can afford a team of industrial cleaners,' Edith said.

'Yes, yes, I'm sure he can,' Rufus said, 'but he's always been a man who cared about his community. Good genetics, you see, probably all the way down from when the Pickles family were the main local landowners around here. No history of uprisings, that's for sure. Everyone was perfectly content.'

'That's nice to know.'

'Come on,' Martha hissed. 'Put her out of her misery. She'll be so happy, we won't need to get her anything for Christmas.'

Rufus puffed out his chest. 'Well ... I've got you a job. And a place to live.'

Edith's smile dropped. 'You ... you don't mean—'

'Yes! That's exactly what I mean. Lord Pickles wants someone to move into Trenton Manor for a few weeks, to clear the place out and give it a clean before he puts it on the market. He said it would probably take a couple of months, and he'll pay well for it.' Rufus clapped his hands together. 'Good pay, somewhere to live ... what more could you want?'

Edith could only stare, but as her parents faded, replaced by memories of running past the creepy old manor house in the dark, of dares with friends to climb over the rusting fence, sneak across the overgrown gardens and peer into the dirty, cobwebbed windows, hoping—or not, perhaps—to catch a glimpse of flickering candlelight, she began to understand the full extent of the horror her father was pushing on her.

As children they had called it the House on Hell Hill, which, while not entirely accurate—that section of Maple Tree Lane was on a gentle incline rather than a true hill—it had been a place both of ridicule and to inspire terror through much of her childhood, until finally her group of friends had grown out of it in their early teens, replacing horror walks and moonlit dares with bus rides into Brentwell's small shopping centre and obsessions with teen idols.

Edith drifted back to the present and realised that both her parents were staring at her, their eyes expectant.

'Well?' Rufus said. 'What do you think? It'll sort you out at least until Christmas, give you a bit of breathing space from stuffy old us, and also allow you to save up a little money for a deposit on a new flat. Sounds perfect, doesn't it?'

'It sounds like a nightmare. You know, that place terrified me as a child. And if you think I'm going to go and live there on my own, you have another thing coming—'

Rufus gave a triumphant grin. 'Ah, but you won't be alone, will you? Pickles told me it's not a job someone could do on their own, so I've volunteered Stephanie to go with you.'

Edith just stared, unable to speak. From somewhere behind her came the crunch of boots on gravel.

'Did someone call my name?' Stephanie asked.

6

TRENTON MANOR

'Structurally it's in great shape,' Lord Arnold Pickles said, leaning on a walking stick as he, Edith, Stephanie, and Edith's parents stood by the wrought-iron gates that opened onto the driveway leading through a stand of trees to Trenton Manor. From here, all they could see was one dark corner of the decrepit, Gothic mansion poking out from behind an oak tree leaning too far out into the driveway to be safe. 'I mean, it probably needs a bit of cosmetic work done to the outside, but it's not going to fall down on you or anything.' He gave a little chuckle which sounded more nervous than anything, then suddenly narrowed his eyes in the direction of the house as though daring it to defy him.

'It's charming,' Martha said. 'To have something like that in your family must make you so proud.'

Arnold, a tiny, crinkled relic of a man seemingly as old as the historical marvel in which he lived, puffed out his chest like a geriatric robin preparing for one last mating season, then abruptly gave a deflating wheeze as though his lungs could no longer sustain it.

'Yes, yes, it's a jewel for sure. It was my great-grandfather, Julius, of course, to whom it was bequeathed by the local lord in this area, whose family had owned it for generations, but who, sadly, had no heirs. Our family did our best to maintain it, of course, my poor son and his dear wife treating it as a family home for a while, but the money just isn't there for the upkeep anymore, hence the reason for sale.'

'You weren't tempted to donate it to a historical charity?' Rufus said.

'Those … bloodsuckers … no,' Arnold said. 'I'd rather poke out my eyes.' He gave another dry, wheezing chuckle. 'Charity begins at home, as they say.'

Rufus nodded in agreement. 'You're echoing my thoughts, dear sir. And from home it spreads to the local community, which is why we're so pleased you've given my daughter here the opportunity to work for you.'

'Well, she looks like a powerful lass,' Arnold said, turning to Stephanie and attempting a wink that only covered his eye halfway.

Rufus just looked amused, then gave Edith an apologetic shrug when Arnold turned back to the house.

'I expect it'll take you a month or more,' the old man said. 'What I require is a complete clear-out. My grandson and I went through the rooms and labelled what needs to go and what needs to stay. The vast majority is for the tip, I'm afraid. After that, the place needs a comprehensive clean. I'm afraid my son—God rest his soul—was a bit of a hoarder.'

'I'm sorry,' Rufus said.

'What for? The idiot gambled away half the family fortune. If a lion hadn't taken him out, I might have done for him myself.' He cleared his throat. 'And the garden will need a bit of cutting back.'

Edith stared through the gates at the overgrown wilderness beyond, wondering how on earth they would manage it. At least Stephanie had the kind of shoulders capable of handling a chainsaw.

'Ideally I'd like it all finished by December,' Arnold said. 'The Christmas market is perfect for selling mansions. Who doesn't want a new house for Christmas?'

Martha and Rufus both chuckled along with him. Edith sighed. Stephanie just frowned and stared through the wrought-iron gates.

'So, you can start right away?' Arnold said, tapping his walking stick on a stone wall almost buried by weeds. 'Of course, with the house opened up and in the process of being cleaned, it'll be vulnerable to trespassers and possible vandals. I'd very much like it if you could live on-site while you undertake your work.'

'That won't be a problem,' Rufus said quickly, loud enough to make Edith's reactionary 'No way!' sound like a strangled cough.

'My daughter and her friend will keep your house safe,' Martha said, making a point of patting Edith on the arm. 'And they'll have the job done on time, I'm sure.'

'Right, well, I'll give you a call later with some further details,' Arnold said. 'A pleasure doing business.'

Before anyone could respond, he turned and hobbled over to a limousine-sized taxi waiting by the road, its engine idling. A driver, wearing sunglasses despite the grey sky, opened the back door for him, then climbed back into the car. It made an awkward U-turn, then sped off.

'Well, that's sorted,' Rufus said. 'Who's for lunch?'

'Fieldy's going to be angry,' Stephanie said, still peering through the gates.

'What?'

'When we cut down that grass, Fieldy's going to be angry.'

~

'I'm not doing it.' Edith prodded a finger at the scribbled writing on Martha's notepad. 'Are you having a laugh? He's only paying us a couple of quid over minimum wage. It's daylight robbery.'

'Oh come on, dear, there's an overnight allowance, and you get a stipend for expenses.'

'Ten pounds a night to sleep in that horrible place, and ten pounds a day for food and drinks. I'd probably earn more at Butlins.'

'Yes, dear, but they're not hiring at this time of year, are they?'

'Mum, I used to have nightmares about that place.'

'Don't be so dramatic. And you'll have Stephanie for company.'

'You keep her locked in her room at night,' Edith hissed, lowering her voice in case Stephanie was hiding in a nearby cupboard or behind the living room curtains.

'I'm glad you've got over all this "my room", "her room" business.'

'Mum—'

'And I imagine there are plenty of lockable doors in a house like that.' She grinned. 'Probably with those massive old keys. You know, I saw a job lot of those for sale online the other day. Do you reckon there's a market for restoring them? Or perhaps making them into fashionable pendants for weird kids?'

Edith grimaced. 'You'll need more room in the cellar.'

'Oh, I'll have plenty now you're moving into Trenton Manor. Just think, it'll be like being a Medieval princess.'

'I'm sure it'll be exactly like that.'

~

In the end, Edith argued herself out. She had nowhere to live, no money, and no job. After one more sleepless night among the horrors of her parents' cellar, she packed her suitcase and loaded it into the back of Rufus's transit van, then climbed into the front, squeezed between her dad and Stephanie.

'You two must be so excited,' Rufus said. 'It must be like going on an adventure.'

'It's only half a mile up the road,' Edith said. 'Don't worry, we'll pop round for tea all the time.'

'Ah, yeah, that might be a problem.'

'What?'

Rufus looked pained as he turned the van out onto the road. 'Well, your mother and I have decided to … take a bit of a holiday.'

Edith felt like she was being repeatedly slapped in the face. 'A holiday? Where?'

'Just over to France. We found a nice holistic retreat in the Alps. Since you two were both moving out, we thought you wouldn't need us around. It's kind of a health place, but more than that, it's an opportunity to both grow internally and externally, if you know what I mean.' He grinned. 'I'll be handing out a whole load of business cards.'

'Not much good it'll do giving them out in the south of France,' Edith said.

Rufus tapped the steering wheel. 'That's not very visionary, is it? What about when those people come on holiday over here, and really need to get a little Soulfree into their lives?'

Edith sighed. 'Go for it, Dad. Wait—hang on a minute. If you're moving out, why can't Stephanie and I just live in your house? Like you said, it's only five minutes from Trenton Manor.'

The triumphant look on Rufus's face was again dashed, replaced by an awkward grimace. 'Ah, well, you see, we've already put it out on short-term rental. We've got someone moving in this afternoon.'

'That was quick!'

'Yes, well, it's a renter's market, isn't it?'

Edith could only shake her head. 'I suppose so. What about Ellen's room?'

'We'll be locking that up. It's out of bounds. They can do what they like in the rest of the house. If you get a chance, could you pop round and check they're sticking to the rules? Ah, here we are.'

The van pulled up outside the gates of Trenton Manor and came to a lurching stop. Edith tried to swallow down a terrible sinking feeling as she peered through the wrought-iron gates at the overgrown gardens, and the corner of the ancient mansion beyond, all of her childhood fears coming back to haunt her. She was still staring when Stephanie let out a sudden gasp and jerked sideways, nearly crushing Edith against the seat.

'He's here! Oh my goodness, he's here!'

'Who?'

'Fieldy!'

She pointed out of the van window. On top of the hedge, a poorly constructed straw man stuck out from between two bushes. One wonky arm appeared to be pointing towards them.

Stephanie was hyperventilating. Edith shoved her dad, trying to get him to open the door and relieve the pressure a little, but Rufus just laughed.

'Oh my God, sorry about that. It was your mother's idea. Just a little prank. She thought it would cheer you up a bit.'

Stephanie was sobbing, struggling to breathe. Rufus finally got the message and opened the door, climbing out to allow Edith to slide away from Stephanie.

'Right, we'd better get your stuff unpacked,' Rufus said, seemingly oblivious to the surrounding drama. 'Otherwise, your mother and I might miss our plane.'

7

A NEW HOME

Stephanie calmed down a little after they had pulled the effigy out of the hedge and found that it was, in fact, just a few bundles of straw with a face scribbled on it in orange marker pen. They propped the fake Fieldy up by the side of the gates, and with a twist of straw when Stephanie wasn't looking, Edith changed his expression to one of anger, perhaps to ward off any potential thieves.

To the best of her memory, Edith had learned to swim wearing armbands in the baby pool at Brentwell Leisure Centre, gently eased into the notion of moving safely through water by herself without any need for trauma or other brutal lessons in the harshness of the real world. However, had her parents always harboured the guilty desire to drop her in at the deep end, they had belatedly done a pretty good job.

Lord Pickles was paying Edith and Stephanie in cash, no doubt as a way to protect his dwindling fortune from a little more tax, promised by five o'clock every Friday. Martha had packed both of them a lunchbox, given them a flask of coffee each, and now Rufus had delivered the final push, leaving them by the verge outside the crumbling mansion, with no way back. To make matters worse, as Edith pulled out her phone, she found she had no signal. It worked perfectly just up the road at her parents' place, so perhaps this was some other ploy of the mysterious Pickles family to keep the outside world at bay.

She was still lost in the horror of being homeless, nearly broke, and abandoned stray-dog-like by the side of the road when she realised Stephanie was coming towards her with a hand raised. Edith gasped and jerked sideways to avoid the potential slap, caught her foot on a protruding root and found herself sitting on the ground, water from the soggy grass quickly soaking through the back of her jeans.

Stephanie loomed over her, blocking out the sun. Her hand was still outstretched, but the slap remained undelivered. Edith, broken and defeated, had half a mind to tell her to get on with it, but was still too disturbed to speak.

'Sorry,' Stephanie said. 'I just thought I ought to properly introduce myself.'

'I know who you are,' Edith said, finding her voice at last.

'Yes, but it was all a little awkward back there, wasn't it? I mean, at your parents' place. I felt like a bit of an intruder.'

Edith took Stephanie's hand and let the bigger girl jerk her to her feet. She brushed grass off her jeans, but the soggy feeling lingered. She shifted uncomfortably.

'It was a bit of a shock to me, too,' she said, in awe of the strength in Stephanie's arms. Had Stephanie revealed herself as an Olympic powerlifter, Edith wouldn't have been surprised. 'I imagine you could guess that my parents were a bit … scatty, but it was quite the surprise they hadn't told me about you.'

'Or me about you,' Stephanie said. 'Or your sister. I wondered why they kept that door locked. I tried to pick it a couple of times, but I'm not good with cam locks. They're one of the hardest types to crack.'

'Is that right?'

Stephanie gave a shy smile. 'You must think I'm a freak,' she said. 'I mean … my condition.'

'Ah … I don't really know much about it.'

Stephanie looked down at her hands, then reached into her pocket. 'It just happens sometimes,' she said. 'I can't help it.' She pulled out something fluffy and rigid. Edith stared. It was one of the squirrels that had been in the tank beside her bed. It looked tiny in Stephanie's hand, a little bowler hat stitched to its head, a tiny dried paw holding a teacup up in an eternal toast.

'You….'

'I'm sorry,' Stephanie said. 'I was careful not to wake you. The cabinet lid was taped down but I used a kitchen knife to cut through it.'

She walked over to the hedge and put the little squirrel down next to Fieldy. Frowning at the way Edith had altered Fieldy's mouth to make him look angry, she said, 'Hopefully a friend will make him feel better.'

Edith was still reeling from the shock that Stephanie had come into her room in the night and stood over her with a kitchen knife, despite both the bedroom door and the cellar door having been locked.

'How on earth did you do it?' she said.

Stephanie looked down at the ground. She was easily six-three, and towered over Edith, who was five-six only on tiptoe. Her shoulders slumped, and Edith regretted the question, but it was too late now.

'I just loosened the lower hinge a little and jostled the door until the bolt slid back,' she said. 'Yours was easy. The key was hanging up in the kitchen.' She sighed. 'It wasn't even a challenge.'

Edith turned to the gate to Trenton Manor. 'I don't suppose you know how to open those?'

Stephanie pulled a huge cast-iron key out of her other pocket. 'I took this from Lord Pickles,' she said, again sounding sad as though she hated her own actions.

'Well, let's try it then,' Edith said, walking up to the gate that loomed over her head. Vines had encircled its bars near to the hinges, and rust had bled down the arch of spikes along the top as though warning away any potential trespassers.

Stephanie put the key into the lock and gave it a sharp twist. With a crack, the end broke off. Stephanie stared at it for a moment, then let it fall to the ground.

'Oh dear,' she said. 'I'm such a freak.'

Secretly Edith was beginning to agree, and had already decided to insist on separate rooms, where she would barricade herself in at night, but saying so wouldn't help their situation. She reached down and picked up the head of the key, which had sheared right off the shaft.

'Look, it was mostly rusted through.' She gave the gates a shake, and they creaked in response. Another harder shake, and the key shaft jostled far enough out of the lock that Edith was able to prise it free with her fingers.

'No harm done,' she said. 'We'll just have to … tape it?'

Stephanie said nothing. Edith half expected her to start screaming and suddenly run off down the road, or alternatively grab hold of the gate and rip it off its hinges with a primal shriek of rage. When Stephanie did nothing except stare at the floor, Edith reached out and patted her shoulder.

'It's all right,' she said. 'We'll just have to climb over the wall. Perhaps we can open it from the other side.'

Stephanie brightened up at this idea, particularly when Edith suggested she give her a leg up. With Stephanie lifting her upwards with no more trouble than a librarian putting a book back on a shelf, she was able to get on top of the wall and jump down into the weeds on the other side.

As she waded through the long grass, a couple of rabbits scattered out of her way and raced up the driveway. Stepping out on to a gravel drive nearly buried in weeds, she glanced down at her jeans, worried about ticks. Through the bars, Stephanie waited, a glum look on her face, looking for all the world like a prisoner just beginning a life sentence.

At the back of the gates, a bolt sank into a tube buried in the ground. Edith tugged it out of an accumulation of dirt and weeds, then pulled on the gates. To her surprise, they began to open with a rusty screech, only to get stuck again, the gap between not yet big enough for a person to squeeze through.ff

'Stephanie? Can you give me a hand?'

The big girl looked up. Understanding the situation, she narrowed her eyes, dropped her shoulder, then charged at the gates, like a prop forward rushing for the try line. The gates resisted only a moment before swinging open. Stephanie stood up straight, and for a moment a look of triumph passed across her face.

'Nice one,' Edith said. 'We're inside. Now let's see if we can get into the actual house.'

They carried their bags through the weeds along the driveway that arced between two lines of trees to a courtyard at the front of the manor. The closer they got, the more impressive it became, rising up out of the overgrown bushes and flowerbeds that surrounded it like a cross between Sleeping Beauty's castle and a Medieval cathedral.

Everything was grey stone, arched windows, steeply pitched slate roofs. The entrance was one storey, but the building appeared tiered, with a second storey visible further back, then a third at the rear, its roof topped by stone spires, alcoved balconies, tall chimneys. Edith could imagine a princess living here in exile, perhaps dying here even, her ghost left to haunt the vaulted halls and corridors for all eternity.

'Look at the trees,' Stephanie said, her voice so abrupt it made Edith jump.

'The trees?'

Stephanie pointed. A paved path, weeds rising between the flagstones, surrounded the house. Along the edge of the garden, trees rose nearly as high as the house: oaks, sycamores, beeches. Their leaves, turned golden orange, red and brown, fluttered over the house with each gust of wind.

'It's beautiful,' Stephanie said.

Edith couldn't help but smile. 'Yes,' she said. 'It is.'

'Do you think it's haunted?'

Edith's smile dropped. 'I hope not,' she said.

'It ought to be,' Stephanie answered, still watching the leaves swirling in the wind. 'It would be appropriate, don't you think?'

8

ON THE INSIDE

Unlike the front gate, they had no difficulty getting into the house itself with the key Arnold had provided. As they walked through a flagstone porch into the entrance hall, Edith looked around, eyes wide, breath catching in her throat. The electricity worked, and now lights fitted into wall alcoves gave the lower part of the hall a dim, orange glow, while clerestory windows higher up in the wall let in natural light.

What might have once been a grand entrance hall, however, was ruined somewhat by the presence of uncountable numbers of stacked cardboard boxes. Many of them looked water damaged, as though they had been left out in the rain, long enough ago that there had been time for spiders to claim them, draping each one in a curtain of ancient, wispy spiderwebs.

'I hate spiders,' Stephanie muttered.

Edith walked over to the nearest box and nudged a corner of ripped cardboard away with her shoe, revealing the contents inside.

'It looks like old magazines,' she said. 'Someone in the

Pickles family must have had a real reading habit though. Seriously, what are we supposed to do with all this stuff?'

They wandered deeper into the house, passing room after room in which the original splendour had been ruined by piles of boxes, stacked furniture, heaped appliances and in one room, car parts, none of which looked to have been made for any car built after 1950. As they stared through one elegant, vaulted doorway into a room filled with incongruous modern office furniture stacked and partly covered with sheets, Edith let out a sigh.

'If you have a habit of stealing, you'll have plenty of choice here,' she said, glancing at Stephanie.

'It doesn't work like that.'

Edith had meant it as a joke, but as Stephanie's shoulders slumped, she felt a pang of guilt.

'Sorry, I didn't mean it like it sounded.'

'I'm not a petty thief,' Stephanie said.

'I know; it's just—'

'You don't know,' Stephanie said with the most conviction Edith thought she'd ever heard out of the other girl. 'I think I'll make a start on the garden.'

Without another word, Stephanie turned and walked back towards the entrance, leaving Edith behind. Edith opened her mouth to apologise again, then decided to leave it. She only risked digging herself a bigger hole, and if Stephanie was about to arm herself with a shovel, it might be a good idea to keep her mouth shut. After all, only her parents, Lord Pickles, and Stephanie knew she was here. How easy it would be for Stephanie to invent a story about how Edith had given up on their job and run off back to Brentwell. Buried among so much junk, no one would ever find her body—

The sudden shriek of a cuckoo clock nearly gave her a heart attack. On the wall nearby hung a sheet, something giving it regular prods from the other side, each accompanied by a loud 'cuckoo-cuckoo!'. Edith reached up and pulled the sheet down, expecting to see a pretty coloured bird chiming the hour out of the door of a brightly painted wooden clock, but to her horror the bird's head was twisted around as though having been throttled, its beak pointing up at the ceiling, a piece of wire poking out of its neck. As it chimed for an eleventh and final time, she was happy to see the little doors close over the monster. Certain it wasn't going to torment her for at least another hour, she slowly hooked the sheet back over the top.

The one thing it had done—apart from scare her half to death—was remind her of the time. It had taken a while to get over the gate and into the house, and a cup of coffee would probably solve, or at least ease, a lot of problems. Although her mother had given them both a flask, she had never liked the plasticky taste and had brought a couple of sachets of instant just in case there was a kitchen in working order somewhere in this place. With a renewed sense of purpose, she went off in search of one.

The ground floor seemed to stretch for miles. Edith wandered through room after room, down narrow corridors where only threadbare strips of faded carpet held back the cold stone. The place had at least been modernised from the Dark Ages, with the installation of electric lights and radiators set into stone alcoves where their effect would likely be minimal, but it still mostly resembled a mothballed museum. When she finally found the kitchen down a set of steps in the middle of the ground floor, her heart only sank further. There was no modern cooker, only an old, woodfired range, which looked like it would take longer to light than it would to cook anything.

Not that there was anything to eat. To her complete surprise, hidden behind a curtain in a corner alcove she found a modern fridge-freezer, but in a way, she was relieved to open it and not find body parts wrapped in plastic or the decomposing severed head of a bull; instead, she found nothing at all. In fact, it wasn't even turned on, a situation she quickly rectified despite having nothing to put inside.

Things began to look up even further when she found an old-fashioned metal kettle hanging from a rail that was a good boil away from being clean enough to use. The stiff taps over a sink large enough to wash a small cow spluttered at first before expelling a slow trickle of brown, grimy water, but the fact they worked at all was enough to encourage Edith, so she left them running while digging some firelighters out of a store cupboard. Soon, much to her amazement, she had a small fire burning inside the range, and water boiling in the kettle.

She had no milk, but that was the least of their problems. She also had no cups other than the little plastic one with her flask and a few huge pewter mugs hanging from the ceiling, cobweb-draped and dusty, but she had hot water, and she had instant coffee.

Nearly there. She got down a couple of the mugs, and scrubbed them out in the sink as best she could, hoping the boiling water would kill off any prehistoric bacteria that might have survived her cleaning attempt. Then, with two full tankards of black coffee in hand, she turned around, intending to go off in search of Stephanie.

A masked figure loomed in the doorway, a chainsaw in one hand: Michael Myers and Jason Voorhees rolled into one. Edith let out a horrified shriek and dropped both mugs, coffee splashing across the floor.

'Stephanie! What on earth are you doing?' she cried, stepping back from the puddle of coffee. 'You scared me half to … death.'

Stephanie lifted her free hand and lowered her mask. 'I'm sorry,' she said, looking down at the floor. 'I just came to tell you that I found a pond. It even has fish in it.'

Edith's heart was still hammering. She wanted to be sorry, but things had been building and building and building, and she felt like a kettle ready to whistle. With a cry of frustration, she kicked out at the nearest tankard, sending it hurtling across the kitchen, where it bounced against the stone wall. She swung at the other one, and it struck the metal front of the sink with a clang.

With nothing else in reach that was moveable, she stamped her foot and punched her sides with her fists.

Only as the sudden expulsion of anger relented, did she realise Stephanie was still standing there, watching her.

'I think you have anger management issues,' Stephanie said.

Edith couldn't help but smile. 'Is it that obvious?'

'That was an impressive meltdown.'

'Were you scared?'

Stephanie shook her head, and a small smile appeared on her face. 'No,' she said. 'I'm holding a chainsaw.'

∼

After mopping up the spillage and retrieving the mugs Edith had booted across the floor, they took their flasks and sat down on a bench at a long table, its surface seemingly made out of one giant slice of wood.

'Coffee,' Edith said, unscrewing the cup-lid. 'This will have to do until the kettle boils again.'

'Sorry again about scaring you.'

'It's all right. We're surviving, aren't we?'

'So far, so good.'

Even though Edith had never liked coffee out of a

flask, it was better than nothing. The moment she unscrewed the cap, however, she realised something was amiss. She poured some of the liquid out and stared at it in horror.

'She told me it was coffee. I saw her making it. Look, this isn't coffee. It's some kind of herbal tea.'

Stephanie unscrewed her flask and poured a little into the cup. 'Same,' she said. 'It smells like nettle and peppermint. Your parents are a little New Age, aren't they?'

'They never used to be. They got through more coffee than the average Costa. I think they're probably going through a midlife crisis.'

'Maybe Fieldy doesn't like it. Your dad told me that He prefers everything to be locally grown.'

'Fieldy.' Edith sighed. 'Maybe. You know that's a load of rubbish, don't you?'

The corner of Stephanie's lip twitched just enough. 'No. I think it's all true.'

Despite her fearsome height, size and propensity to invoke terror, Edith realised she was warming to Stephanie. The girl might have issues, but then so did she.

'It must have been pretty tricky living with them. It wasn't in my plans to move home.'

'You just needed a safety net. I know.' Stephanie's smile widened just a little more. 'They've been kind to me. I mean, it wasn't quite what I expected, but it was all right. It was a surprise they didn't tell me about you or Ellen.'

'Especially about Ellen,' Edith said. 'The jewel in the Davies crown. I'm surprised they didn't fill your evenings by talking about her and all her achievements for hours on end. They used to be so bad that one of my boyfriends developed an obsession with her. He dumped me and went off to America to profess his undying love.'

'Did he actually do that?'

'Yes. He got arrested for stalking her and then deported. She chose not to press charges, and now he works in Wrights up on the Brentwell road, in the garden furniture department.'

Stephanie's eyebrows lifted. 'Oh, you don't mean Harry?'

Edith smiled. 'Harry Anderson. That's him. You know him?'

'Yes, he sold my stepmother a set of patio chairs. He was telling us about this new drama that had just come out. The Rain Box, something like that.'

'The Rain Vault. It's about a group of kids who get washed down a drain in a storm and discover a secret world underneath their city. My sister wrote it.'

'It must be weird having a famous sister.'

'I'd like to say you get used to it, but you don't, not really. She always seems to be doing something new, something interesting. Winning this or that, meeting this or that famous person. And my parents love to tell me all about it.'

'Huh. That must get tiring.'

'It's why I keep them at arm's length. Or at least I did. I once tried to prove myself worthy of my family's name by doing a bit of open mic stand-up comedy at university. I was rubbish at it, though.' Edith sighed and poured a little more of the nettle and peppermint tea into her cup. It was pleasant enough, but it was too dainty, not enough to really pick her up.

'You shouldn't give up,' Stephanie said. 'You never know what might happen.'

'Not much, unfortunately,' Edith said. 'Come on, we need more coffee. If we walk back into Willow River we can get some from the supermarket.'

'I think there are some cattle roaming free on the grounds,' Stephanie said. 'I saw a few while I was clearing around the pond. If we corner one, perhaps we can milk it.'

'Are you serious?'

Again, that tiny twitch of Stephanie's lips. 'No,' she said. 'But there's a Spar in Trenton. That's much closer than Willow River.'

'Trenton village?'

'Yes, it's just up the road.'

'Is there anything there? I don't think I've ever even been through it.'

'A shop, a church. A pub.'

Edith lifted an eyebrow. 'A pub, you say? Do you think it's too early to celebrate our survival so far?'

Stephanie watched her, and the smile that occasionally threatened to break out, finally spread across her face.

'No,' she said. 'I don't think it's too early at all.'

9
TRENTON

Trenton was one of those villages dotting the British countryside that suffered from being neither on a main road, nor the location of anything significant. A single lonely sign on the road that connected Bathwater, Birch Valley, and Willow River to Brentwell indicated 'Trenton 2¼', but to the best of her memory Edith had passed the junction perhaps a million times without ever having taken it. Trenton Manor was on a private road that looped back to the main road, but as they waded through the long grass and weeds that had once been a rear lawn, they came to a small stone arch harbouring a rusted, weed-choked gate that opened directly onto the narrow, winding Trenton road. Any passer-by could be forgiven for thinking that the gate was a curio, perhaps the entrance to some long-demolished building, with Trenton Manor itself out of sight in the valley and screened by trees, but it wouldn't have mattered anyway because no one ever seemed to go to Trenton. It was a lost little place, a word on a map, a church spire poking out of a valley, a name on a road sign no one ever gave a second glance.

Now, Edith and Stephanie found themselves trudging down a road barely wide enough for a single car, let alone two, to pass, tall hedgerows on either side broken only by the occasional field entrance.

'I always wondered why they called this Maple Tree Lane,' Edith said. 'There aren't any maples on it, just hedges.'

'You have to wait,' Stephanie said, as they passed a field gate from which they could see the church spire in the valley, definitely larger than it had been the last time they had caught a glimpse. 'There's only a few on the hill, but down in the village there's a whole ring of them.'

'I can't believe I've never been down here before,' Edith said, as they came around a sharp switchback and found the village of Trenton laid out in the valley below them, the maple trees Stephanie had promised making a sweeping arc of red and orange down to the flat valley floor, then following the road out of the valley as it angled uphill on the other side.

The village itself was little more than a cluster of houses on either side of a languid river. A little humpback bridge was the only way across. A couple of narrow roads ended in rings of stone houses, while a church was set among more trees halfway up the hill. On one side of the little bridge was the Spar, with an ancient, thatch-roofed pub on the other, set back from the road behind a gravel car park.

Stephanie smiled. 'Dad used to take me down there when I was little,' she said. 'There's a play area around the back, but I preferred to play in the river. There's a flat part of the bank, which is sandy, like a little beach. We used to dam it, try to catch the fish.'

Edith couldn't remember a time when Stephanie had volunteered so much information in one go. As she glanced at the other girl, she caught Stephanie wiping a tear out of the corner of her eye. She opened her mouth to say something, but before she could think of anything meaningful to say, Stephanie had marched ahead, her huge stride taking her quickly down into the valley. Edith hurried after her, only catching up when Stephanie paused by the little humpback bridge to peer over the edge into the water. A plaque in the middle of the bridge said 1864, which Edith took as the building date, although she guessed the tarmacked road was a later addition.

'Look, you can see trout,' Stephanie said. 'Big ones, too.'

They headed across the bridge to the shop, an ice-cream sign flapping in the breeze outside. Stephanie, getting there before Edith, waited outside, giving Edith an awkward smile. 'It's only open until one today,' she said, nodding at a sign.

Edith checked her watch. It was half past twelve already, and from the look of a couple of picnic tables outside, the pub was already open. By the time they ordered and sat down, the shop would be closed. During the walk she had made a mental shopping list of what they might need to survive until tomorrow, in addition to milk, including such essentials as soap, cream crackers, and a pack of cards. Had she known a little in advance that her parents would be renting their house out from under her, she might have prepared better. As it was, they were at the mercy of this shop in the middle of nowhere.

'We'd better be quick,' she said to Stephanie. 'If you want, you can go and get the drinks in.'

For a moment she thought Stephanie would take her up on the offer, but then the other girl gave a nervous shrug. 'It's okay,' she said. 'We'll go up there together. They might think it a bit weird, you know, if I just go in on my own.'

Edith nodded. While during the heady days of being employed she had been able to keep her head above the financial waters with only a minimum of fuss, her depressingly empty bank account would resemble the Sahara Desert in a drought before long if Stephanie was even more of a financial lost cause than she was. Perhaps the pub wasn't a good idea after all. But then, they'd walked all the way down here; they would need some kind of fuel to get back up the hill.

'Come on, then,' she said, leading the way into a gloomy and cramped village shop. An elderly woman looked up from behind a counter in the far corner with a look of surprise on her face.

'You girls lost?' she muttered, voice cracking a little as though it had been some hours since she had last needed to speak. With the creak of a chair, she rose uncertainly to her feet, body unfolding like a deckchair being opened for a new summer. 'Pretty sure I haven't seen you round here before.'

'We're staying at Trenton Manor,' Edith said. 'We're the … ah, cleaning team.'

'Is that right?' The old woman pushed spectacles up her nose and squinted through the lenses, only for them to slide down again. With a frustrated huff, she took them off and put them down on the counter. 'Old Pickles finally decided to fix the place up, has he?'

'I think he's planning to sell it.'

'Huh. Good luck with that. You'd have to pay me to take one step into that accursed old place. Are you all right over there, dear?'

Stephanie was standing in the corner, back turned, squeezed into a gap between the shelves and the wall. She turned, almost knocking the nearest rack over, making the tins and packets rattle.

'Ah, I was just looking for the chewing gum,' she said.

'It's over here, by the counter, on the chewing gum rack,' the old woman said.

'Right. Thanks.'

Stephanie, needing to move sideways, approached the counter and picked a packet of Wrigleys Spearmint out of the rack.

'Pound,' the old woman said, squinting as she watched Stephanie put a hand into her pocket, pulling out a crumpled ten-pound note. The old woman rang it up on the till and handed Stephanie her change. Just as Stephanie was about to put it into her pocket, she turned and held a hand out to Edith.

'For the rest,' she said.

Edith, who had fully expected Stephanie to be broke, struggled for something to say.

'Um, it's—'

'Jobseekers,' Stephanie said with a shrug.

'Right. I mean—'

'Old Pickles paying you cash in hand, is he?' the woman said with a witchlike cackle. 'Sounds about right for that family. Liars and thieves, the lot of them. Can't expect someone whose family fortune came from fraud to be any better. I'll take that, then you go and get what you want.'

Before Edith could react, she had leaned over the counter and scooped Stephanie's change out of her hand. A couple of coins dropped to the floor, Stephanie nearly knocking over another rack as she bent to pick them up.

The items Edith wanted came to a little more than what the woman had taken from Stephanie, so she added the extra and then promised to get the drinks in when they got to the pub. Stephanie just shrugged, but Edith, who had been employed until yesterday, couldn't help but feel bad about it. As they walked through the pub car park, Stephanie turned away, wandering over to the river, where she stood looking down, one hand pushed into her pocket. As Edith came up behind her, she heard Stephanie sniff.

'They walled it up,' she said, pointing at a riverbank that looked newly constructed, a wall made of stone-filled wire cages. 'The little beach bit, it's gone.'

'I think we'd better get some pints in,' Edith said.

It was warm enough for them to sit outside, so they took a table in the pub garden, overlooking the river, the towering maple trees swaying gently in the breeze, occasionally showering them with red and orange leaves. They were both wondering at the pub's name—The Sparrow Bridge—when a dozen or so of the little birds fluttered down from the trees and began to pick through the leaves at their feet.

Edith ordered fish 'n' chips, Stephanie a steak and ale pie. Edith changed her mind on getting a beer and instead ordered a glass of wine, but to her surprise Stephanie wanted only Coca Cola. As they waited for their food, Edith found her frustration growing. Stephanie was distracted, morose, seemingly lost in the memories of some traumatic past.

'Are you all right?' Edith asked at last. 'You really don't look like you're having much fun. I mean, it's a bit of a weird situation, right? Not what I could have imagined when I got up yesterday and went off to work, but like … it's kind of pretty here, isn't it?'

Stephanie's chest heaved, and Edith thought she might start to cry. She reached into her pocket and took something out, putting it down on the tabletop. Edith stared at a handful of dog-eared postcards, all of them showing the same aerial view of the village in autumn: the bridge and the pub on the left, the church on the right, the maple trees making their sweeping line down through the valley. TRENTON was written in black letters in the bottom right corner, and from the faded look of those at the front of the little stack, they had been sitting in the shop unsold for some years.

'I took them,' Stephanie said, looking down at her hands, then suddenly clenching her fingers, clawing at the tabletop. 'I couldn't help myself.'

10

UNDERSTANDING

While getting drunk might not solve anything, it certainly gave Edith a little more freedom to offer her advice.

'You know you can't just take stuff, don't you?' she said, taking a long sip of her second glass of wine.

Stephanie nodded. 'Of course I know that.'

'We need to take them back, say you forgot you'd picked them up, that we need to pay for them. How many did you steal?'

Stephanie spread out the cards into a fan shape. 'Looks like about thirty-five.'

'Wow, she's going to think you really like it here. Why don't you tell her they were for your old school classmates or something? You know, there's no TV up at that house that I could see, so you have to do something in the evenings, don't you? Why not write postcards?'

Stephanie gave a sad shrug. 'I suppose.'

Edith fell silent as she wondered what they should do with the stolen postcards. Stephanie held them in her hand like a treasured toy, the look on her face suggesting it was one her mother had just ordered her to throw away. Edith stared at her, seeing in her face the look she had often seen on the faces of patients heading into Dr. Woodfield's office. A look that said they needed help.

'You can't help it, can you?' she said quietly, leaning forward. 'I don't really understand it, but that's what it is, isn't it? Kleptomania? You don't want to steal, but you can't stop yourself.'

Stephanie gave a sad nod. 'I … know it's wrong. But it's like I get a … rush. When I get away with it, I mean. Like I've won something. And then a moment later it's over, and I hate myself, but it's too late to go back.'

Edith stared at her. 'I used to work for a therapist,' she said. 'However, she was a total quack. We all knew it. The office was nice and she looked the part, but she didn't really care that much about her patients beyond making sure they paid. I'd see people coming out looking worse than when they went in. I don't know what she was doing, but she wasn't curing people. But I do think it helped them to talk about their problems, even if it was to someone who wasn't really listening.' She leaned forwards again until the cold wood of the bench was pressing into her stomach. 'If you want to tell me, I'll listen.' She smiled. 'I mean, we don't have a television, so what else are we going to do?'

Stephanie nodded at the plastic bag of shopping Edith had bought and gave a little smile. 'Play cards?'

∽

'It first happened after my dad left,' Stephanie said, taking a sip of Coca Cola that had been upgraded with a shot of vodka. 'It's a total cliché, isn't it?'

'Most things are,' Edith agreed, three glasses of wine deep. She picked up a remaining chip and bit off half.

Even cold, it was salty and oily, just as she liked them. 'Why did he leave?'

'He loved me, and he was a great dad, but he was a gambler. The horses mostly, but he'd put money on anything. We had the bailiffs come round once. They cleaned us out, took everything. Even my toys.'

'Seriously?'

Stephanie nodded. 'I was seven or eight years old. They took the dolls out of my hands, put them in a plastic bag. One even smiled at me as though to say sorry. I remember he was huge, looming over me. I was so scared, but his smile made me feel like it was all right. That he was sorry.'

'What happened to your father?'

'He couldn't stop. He disappeared not long after. The house got repossessed. Mum found out he'd emptied our bank accounts. We ended up in a kind of shelter hostel place. I found out years later that my mum wasn't actually my real mum, that my birth mother died when I was too young to remember, and my stepmother—who I'd always thought was my real mum—kind of resented me. She looked after me, but she worked two jobs, so I hardly saw her. I went to school, came home to an empty room.' She shrugged. 'There was a dining hall in the hostel. I ate in there, waited for Mum to come home. Sometimes she'd read me a story; other times she'd be too tired to bother, so I'd read it myself, or just look at the pictures until I fell asleep.'

'I'm so sorry.'

Stephanie shrugged. 'It wasn't as bad as it sounds. Mum got remarried in the end, to Jonathan. He was all right. He adopted me, and I took his name, Madden, mostly to make Mum happy, I suppose. He's never been much of a dad to me, but I can understand that. I'm not the kind of person anyone would be proud of.'

'Don't say that! That's not true!'

'There's no need to shout,' Stephanie said, glancing back over her shoulder at the pub. 'Perhaps we ought to make that your last glass of wine.'

Edith grinned. 'Who are you, my mother?'

Stephanie gave another small smile. 'Don't worry. I could probably carry you back up to the house. You can't weigh more than eight stone.'

'I'm nine and a half, I'll have you know.'

'In that case, I'll let you carry me.'

'I … I'm not sure—'

'I'm joking. Maybe we could call a taxi, or get the landlord to give us a lift up the hill. I haven't seen any other customers.'

Edith lifted her glass. 'Well, since we're bonding, I think we should have one more for the road.'

'I'm not sure how we can justify this as work time to Lord Pickles.'

'Of course we can. We're brainstorming, making a game plan for how to clean that house of his.'

'All right. Well, I think the best way will be to break it down into chunks. Deal with it room by room, maybe.'

Stephanie was far more practical than Edith could have believed. The landlord lent her a pen and paper on which she began to scribble down a list of tasks that could be done without the help of any outside contractors or heavy machinery. Take an inventory of their cleaning materials and gardening tools. Get the kitchen in working order. Change any broken light bulbs. Clear the driveway. Cut the grass. Clean the windows. Clean grout from the bathrooms. Move everything to be thrown away down into the entrance hall. Order a skip, or alternatively hire someone to collect and dispose of the rubbish. Oil the locks.

The list went on and on. Edith tried to concentrate as Stephanie talked through each task, all the while wondering how Stephanie, with such obvious management and organisation skills, had ended up unemployed, lodging with her parents.

'Are you girls all right out here?' the landlord said, as he came out to collect another set of glasses. 'You sure you're not cold? We have a fire inside.'

Edith smiled, but Stephanie shook her head. 'We're all right, thank you,' she said.

'It is getting cold,' Edith said, standing up, swaying worryingly. 'Perhaps we could go in and warm up for a bit before heading back up the hill.'

'No!'

Edith frowned. 'But—'

'I said, no.'

Then, to her surprise, Stephanie pulled a fifty-pound note out of her pocket and handed it to the landlord.

'We'll settle up, if that's okay.'

'If you're sure,' he said. 'I have to say, we don't get many customers at this time of the year, but you two are certainly quite a pair. Didn't you say you were stopping up at Dracula's place for a while? If so, be sure to stop by again. Friday night is open mic night. Either of you sing or play anything?'

Edith shook her head as Stephanie said, 'She does jokes, but I don't do anything.'

'Well, stop by. We only ever get a handful. Be good to see you both again.' He winked. 'Doubled my takings for the week.'

The landlord took their glasses and returned a few

minutes later with their change. As he went back into the pub, Stephanie handed it to Edith.

'This is yours,' she said. 'I took that note out of your purse while you were in the toilet half an hour ago.' She looked down at the table. 'Sorry.'

Edith just smiled. 'It's okay. I had no idea I had a fifty-pound note.'

'It was folded up in the pocket next to a tampon and behind an expired National Trust card.'

'Ah, my emergency money. Well, I suppose this is a bit of an emergency, isn't it?' She stood up again, nearly toppling over. 'Oh dear.'

'I think we'd better get you home,' Stephanie said.

'I don't have a home,' Edith muttered. 'I don't have a home, and I don't have a job. I don't have a boyfriend, and I don't have any money.'

Stephanie just gave her a pained look. 'Do you want a postcard? I have plenty to share.'

~

Somehow they got up the hill. The strenuous climb sent Edith's head into a spin, so by the time they got back to Trenton Manor just before dusk, she felt like she'd drunk double her four glasses of wine.

'You must think I'm a lush,' she said to Stephanie, as the other girl steered her in through the main entrance, then narrowly averted her from crashing into a pile of horse-riding magazines. 'I don't drink very often, you know. Only when I have a ... crisis.'

She hiccupped her way through a little further conversation, Stephanie steering her along the corridor and up a staircase with an ornate metal handrail that was cold enough under her fingers to almost sober her up. At the top of the stairs, Stephanie took her into a room filled with sheeted objects, like irregularly shaped ghosts. With a flourish, she pulled one free, revealing a wire-framed bed that looked more akin to a mental hospital ward than a manor house.

'That'll do,' Stephanie said. 'Just lie on there for a while. That'll help.'

The mattress was hard but the duvet soft. The sheet had kept off the dust, and as Edith lay down, she felt sleep beckoning her.

'I'm sorry,' she muttered as Stephanie, like an attentive nurse, pulled the duvet up to her shoulders.

'What for?'

'For thinking you were weird.' Definitely the wine had got her tongue. Hearing the words externally as though she were having an out-of-body experience, she tried to recall them. 'I didn't … I didn't mean—'

'It's okay,' Stephanie said. 'I am. You know, if there was a medium, I'd definitely be off-centre. You have a rest now.'

～

When Edith woke, the room was filled with long shadows cast by silvery moonlight through the open window. Edith sat up, looking around, at first confused. This wasn't her flat, nor her parent's cellar. As realisation dawned, she climbed out of bed, standing uncertainly among the amorphous sheet-covered shadows.

She still wore her clothes, but Stephanie had removed her shoes. The air was bitingly cold on her hands and feet, the back of her neck. Needing to pee, she went to the door and peered out. Stairs to her right descended into darkness. To her left, a long, baroque corridor stretched away, lit only by a single lamp someone—she hoped it was Stephanie—had left on a table halfway along. With there being no question about descending into the dark, she walked to the light, which she found had been placed outside a small bathroom. Leaving the door open to give her some light, Edith went in and relieved herself, grateful that someone—again, she hoped it was Stephanie and not someone else secretly living here whom they hadn't met yet —had thought to put a new toilet roll in the holder.

In the lamplight, her watch told her it was a little after one o'clock in the morning. She started going back towards her room, the only sound the gentle padding of her feet on the carpet. Halfway there, she paused, stopping and holding her breath, sure she could hear something else, a gentle soughing sound, like the wind blowing through a window someone had left open.

She turned and walked back up the corridor, only prepared to go as far as the light would let her. Ghosts were obviously a load of rubbish, but if there was somewhere that had a chance of changing her opinion, it was here in this gloomy old mansion.

The source of the sound came from a room at the very end of the corridor, right where the light was about to peter out. Another bedroom, the door left ajar. Moonlight streamed in through a tall bay window, illuminating a figure lying on the bed. Stephanie's huge frame took up most of it, one knee bent, one foot hanging over the wire frame at the end. The cover exposed her shoulders, the t-shirt she wore as her back lifted up and down, snoring gently, the source of the sound. Edith smiled, went to close the door a little, then realised Stephanie, lying on her side, held something in her hand as it stuck out above the floor.

She frowned. A small rectangle, like a postcard. The moonlight left the message side in shadow, and Edith didn't want to wake Stephanie, so she backed silently out of the room and returned to her own bedroom.

With nothing else to do, perhaps Stephanie had decided to write some postcards after all, although from the way she had been lying, it looked as though she had been reading it.

Never mind. When they returned them in the morning —as Edith intended—the shopkeeper probably wouldn't notice one missing.

Starting to feel the chill creeping under her clothes, Edith headed back to bed.

11

DOWN TO BUSINESS

'Right, today's task is to make this place semi-habitable,' Edith said, watching Stephanie from across the table, two steaming pewter mugs of coffee between them. 'That means: kitchen, bathroom, bedrooms.'

'Patio,' Stephanie said with a little smile. 'So that we can drink coffee outside.'

'Great idea. Why don't we do that first? It's warm outside, but it's so cold inside the house. I don't know how anyone could stand living here.'

'They need to upgrade the heating for sure,' Stephanie said. 'It was freezing last night.'

Edith suddenly had a flashback to her midnight walk. 'Thanks for putting that lamp on in the hall,' she said. 'It was you, wasn't it?'

'No,' Stephanie said, shaking her head, sending a bolt of horror striking through Edith's heart, before giving a little smile and adding, 'Yes, of course it was me.'

'Thank God for that,' Edith said with a sigh of relief. 'And thanks for putting me to bed. I had to get up in the night, to use the loo. I … ah, saw it looked like you were … uh … writing those postcards.'

Stephanie shook her head. 'No, I left them downstairs, by the door.' She gave Edith a resolute smile. 'I'm going to do it, you know. I'm going to go back to that shop today and return them.'

'Oh, right. I thought I saw you had one in your room. Not that I was spying or anything, but I heard a noise and I went to look and … you know.'

Stephanie looked confused, then gave a quick nod. 'I … oh.' She shook her head, looking away. 'It's nothing. Shall we get started on that patio?'

~

It was arduous work, and the November chill was a constant companion, even if the sky stayed clear and bright, and the patio they had chosen to work on first faced south, meaning it had the sun all day long. What had once been a wide area of quartz gravel interspersed with paving stone sections and raised flowerbeds was now an overgrown wilderness. They started by clearing the paved sections, making them into islands among the waist-high weeds. In the years since the property had been abandoned, a number of saplings had grown up out of the gravel, some reaching several feet in height and a couple of inches in thickness. Edith, giving up on digging one out with a spade, wiped sweat off her brow and turned to Stephanie, who was pulling weeds out from under a row of raised patio stones, a pile of muddy roots in a wheelbarrow beside her.

'I don't think I'll ever get this thing out,' Edith said. 'And there are loads of them. Do you think we should just kind of feature these in, or cut them with that chainsaw you found?'

Stephanie gave a sheepish grin. 'What chainsaw?'

'Yesterday, in the kitchen—'

'It was on … um, short-term loan from the timber merchant down the road,' Stephanie said. 'I returned it this morning … before the place opened.'

Edith nodded. 'Ah, I … see. Oh well, so how about we try to work these trees into a new design?'

'Good idea,' Stephanie said.

～

By lunchtime they had managed to clear the weeds from a section of the patio big enough for a potential game of badminton—although they only had a single crusty, stringless racquet for which they had found meshed in a patch of brambles—repaired an old bench well enough to take their weight, and pruned enough flowerbeds back to make it clear that the place had once been quite pleasant, even if it had fallen into a shadow of its former self. Together, they made spaghetti in the kitchen and then took it outside to eat, although by the time they had carried it up the gloomy corridor from the kitchen and all the way outside, it was almost cold.

'We need to get some of those covers you put over food in posh restaurants,' Stephanie said. 'Do you think they sell them in the shop down in Trenton?'

Edith shrugged. 'I doubt it, but we could go and check later.' She smiled. 'You know, when we take those postcards back.'

Stephanie nodded. 'I haven't forgotten, although I'm trying to. Let's make a list of other things we need first, so you can at least get them before you get banned and I get arrested.'

'You won't get arrested over a few postcards,' Edith said with a grin, but the look on Stephanie's face suggested she thought otherwise.

'Stealing is stealing,' Stephanie said.

'Is that why you can't get a job?' Edith asked. 'You've been prosecuted?'

Stephanie grimaced and wiped a tear out of her eye. 'I have a criminal record as long as some of this grass,' she said. 'I've been done for shoplifting six times.'

'Seriously?'

Stephanie nodded. 'Mostly in Exeter, but I got cautioned after I stole some lawnmower blades out of Wright's on the Brentwell Road. They didn't press charges because they knew me.'

'Lawnmower blades? Why?'

Stephanie sighed. 'I don't even know anyone with a lawnmower. They were a really weird shape and I wanted to see if I could get away with it. They set off a metal detector by the doors. I didn't think they were the right kind of metal.'

She looked down at the tabletop, tracing lines in the lichen with a finger. Edith watched her for a moment, the pain obvious in Stephanie's furrowed brow. She wished there was something she could do.

'Do you know why you do it?' she asked quietly. 'The stealing, I mean?'

Stephanie shook her head, and when she spoke, she sounded on the verge of tears. 'I just get this urge. I can't control it. I know it's the wrong thing to do, but I just can't help myself.'

'Do you think it's something related to your father leaving? Or maybe something genetic?'

'I don't know. When I see something that I want, I just … I have to have it. And then as soon as I've got it, I hate myself. All the bad feelings come back, all the guilt, the self-loathing. I can't look at myself in the mirror.'

Edith cocked her head. 'Is that what the glasses are about? The hair?' She smiled. 'I can understand the jumper because it's freezing, but … you know, I don't think you should hate yourself. In fact, I think you should learn to do the opposite.' She tapped the tabletop with her hand. 'Look, I don't want to sound like a psychiatrist, and I don't want to act like it's something trivial because it's not, but you did a great impression of my mother yesterday, putting me to bed and all that, so how about I give you a bit of payback and do the doctorly thing?'

'I don't understand.'

Edith reached into her pocket, fumbled around and found a hairband at the bottom. She picked a couple of pieces of fluff off it, grinned, and held it out. 'Here. Put your hair back.'

'I don't know….'

'Just do it. It's only the two of us here. No one's going to see, are they?'

'I will.'

'Have you seen any mirrors in this place? I mean, there might be one under a sheet somewhere, but they're not exactly all over, are they?'

'All right.'

Stephanie pulled the curtains of hair back from her face and put it up in a ponytail. Edith lifted an eyebrow. Like a flower opening out for the first time, Stephanie had suddenly bloomed, and with a bit of make-up would turn plenty of heads, especially those of Norwegian lumberjacks, heavyweight boxers, pro wrestlers, and anyone else likely to have a height advantage.

'That's much better. Do you have contacts or anything?'

Stephanie reached up and took off her glasses. 'I don't even need them,' she said, putting them down on the table. 'I took them from an optician's shop on Brentwell High Street and I've been wearing them ever since. They're just a frame sample with clear plastic lenses.'

'Perhaps leave them for a while; see how you feel.'

'Do you think so?'

'Yes, why not? Don't you feel better? You already look like you're not hiding anymore.'

'I'm cold.'

'Yeah, we might need to sort out a couple of hats. Right, now for the doctor bit. You told me you get uncontrollable urges to steal. Maybe that's like when you're eating chocolates or something, and you can't resist another one.'

'Something like that, but it's stronger.'

'How about if you think of something to do whenever you get the urge to take something, you know, as a kind of warning to yourself?'

'Like what?'

Edith shrugged. 'I don't know … why don't you … ah … do a chicken gesture?'

It was the first thing that came to mind, something she had done at random during the few regrettable occasions she had done stand-up comedy at university. Unlike most of her jokes, it had always gained a laugh.

'Are you serious?'

'It might help. It'll remind you not to steal. If you just do a few clucks or whatever, it'll be a like a warning to yourself.'

'I'll look like an idiot.'

'Just try it a couple of times.'

Stephanie nodded. 'All right. I'll try.'

'I don't want to embarrass you or anything. I'm only trying to help.'

'I know.' Stephanie rubbed her hands together. 'Right. What's next on the list?'

'I reckon we should do a bit inside the house for a while. Find out what's under all those sheets in the bedrooms.'

'Good idea.'

They got back to work. The sheets turned out to reveal furniture of all kinds and from multiple time periods. The room Stephanie had chosen as her bedroom contained a dresser so crusty and ornate that it could have serviced Queen Victoria, while the one in Edith's room came from IKEA and contained a built-in phone charger. Elsewhere, they found cabinets filled with old vases, sports trophies from a hundred years ago, and a few stuffed game birds, but not nearly as many as Martha had assembled. They also found a grand piano, the lid of which Stephanie lifted just long enough to press a single key before dropping it back down again.

'Do you play?' Edith asked.

Stephanie shrugged. 'Not really. I had a few lessons as a kid. There was one in the hostel. One of the helpers used to show me a tune or two while I was waiting for Mum to come back from work.'

'Why don't you have a go?' Edith said. 'I wish I could play something. Ellen got lessons when we were kids, but Mum always said I wasn't interested. I don't ever remember being asked.'

'Maybe sometime,' Stephanie said. 'We should get this cleaning done.'

The bathroom between their rooms proved less enjoyable to clean than the bedrooms, with a significant number of spiders and other insects present, both living and dead. Stephanie came across as fearless but screamed like a child when she looked into an alcove and took a spiderweb full in the face. Afterwards, they decided to retreat outside for an afternoon coffee.

They were sitting on the patio enjoying the last of the day's warmth, the sun dipping into the tallest branches of the trees to the west, making the remaining leaves glitter red and gold, when Stephanie sat up sharply, eyes flicking around.

'What is it?' Edith said.

'Did you hear that?'

'What?'

'The crack of a twig. It sounded like footsteps.'

'It could be one of those cows you said were roaming free.'

'I'm pretty sure they came from a neighbouring field and got in through a gap in the hedge. No, that was definitely footsteps. There it was again. Did you hear it?'

This time Edith had. She stood up, looking around as the cracking of twigs came closer. 'Who's there?' she called.

A figure stepped out from behind a tree, making both of them scream in fright. A man, around thirty, taller than Edith but shorter than Stephanie, lifted a hand and offered a smile of greeting.

'Sorry to intrude,' he said. 'I was around the front but I thought I heard voices.'

'Who are you?' Edith said. 'You know this is private property, don't you?'

'Yes, of course.'

He came a few steps closer, lifting his hands in a gesture of submission. His hair was dark, almost black; his eyes a chestnut brown. He had little dimples in his cheeks when he smiled that made him look rather—

Edith gave a little shake of her head. *What the hell is wrong with me?*

'Uh, we could call the police.'

The man lifted an eyebrow, then pulled a phone out of his pocket and held it up. 'You can borrow mine if you like, but do you know anywhere in the grounds where you can get reception? I can't get anything.'

'We could shout really, really loud,' Edith said. 'Plus, Stephanie here is a pro wrestler.' Stephanie gave a little growl as though for proof. 'You really don't want to mess with us.'

'I have no intention of messing with you. I just wanted to see how you were getting on.' He turned to Stephanie. 'So, you're Stephanie. That must make the mouthy one Edith.'

'Mouthy? You cheeky so-and-so.'

The man spread his arms and gave them a smile wide and smug enough to block the Panama Canal. Even then Edith found herself swaying from side to side, like an iron filing caught in a magnetic pull. 'Sorry, I didn't mean to offend,' the man said. 'Just going on what I can see. My name's James. James Archer. James Archer-Pickles, if you want my full name.'

'Pickles?' Stephanie said. 'As in Lord Arnold Pickles?'

'I'm his grandson,' James said. 'This whole estate belongs to me, or at least it will as soon as Grandfather passes away. Before long I'll be so rich I could make a tree out of money and then pay someone to set fire to it.'

'There's no need to be so smug about it,' Edith said, still smarting from the 'mouthy' comment but unable to keep her eyes off James. 'Not all of us are lucky enough to have rich parents.'

Autumn on Maple Tree Lane

'Not all of us have parents,' James said, dropping his eyes into a puppy-dog expression of despair. 'Both of mine are dead and buried.'

'Oh, well I'm sorry to hear that,' Edith said, wanting to sound sarcastic but at the same time feeling an otherworldly need to put an arm around his shoulders.

'At least you know where they are,' Stephanie said.

James ignored her. 'I was just in the area, and thought I'd come and see how you were getting on,' he said. 'I'm afraid my grandfather has been taken ill, and it's unlikely he'll recover. He's asked me to oversee the tidying up and sale of this place on his behalf.'

'I'll give you a fiver for it,' Edith said, then silently admonished herself for the way he looked hurt.

'Yeah, that's funny. Look, let's be friends. Grandfather hired you to clean the place. How are you getting on? Do you need anything?'

'Well, if you're asking, about twenty more people,' Edith said. 'A couple of industrial vacuums, a skip—'

'A chainsaw,' Stephanie said.

James lifted up a bag and put it on the table. 'I'm afraid I don't have everything you need right now, but I'll put them on a wish list. What I do have right now, is some wire brushes, a couple of packs of refuse bags, some cloths, and a triple-pack of scrubbing sponges.' He held up the last item and grinned. 'Look: buy two, get one free.'

'Thanks,' Edith said, getting a sideways look from Stephanie, before forcing a bit of sarcasm to add, 'I'm sure that'll speed us up through the thirty-eight rooms we haven't started on yet.'

'You'll be fine,' James said. 'Look, I'm staying nearby, so I'll stop by again on Friday for an update. In the meantime, I'll see what I can do about those items you asked for. I can't promise anything. Money's pretty tight, hence the sale. Right, I'd better get back to the Porsche. I'm not keen on leaving it unattended on these country lanes. People always say the cities are full of crime, but they don't know the countryside like we know it, do they?'

'No,' Edith said. 'You have a Porsche?'

'It's only a rental, but I like to travel in style.'

'I need the toilet,' Stephanie said, standing up. Then, as though catching herself, she tucked her hands under her arms and shouted, 'Cluck, cluck! Cluck, cluck, cluck!'

'I think she's having a seizure,' James said.

Edith caught a wide-eyed look from Stephanie and stood up. 'I'll deal with it,' she said, taking Stephanie's arm and steering her towards the house. 'Nice to have met you … James.'

He walked off towards the driveway as Edith led Stephanie around to the entrance.

'Are you all right?' she said, letting go of Stephanie's arm.

Stephanie took a deep breath. 'Phew. That was close. I had an overwhelming urge to just move his car into a field somewhere.' She shook her head. 'I think I'm over it now, though.'

'He was a bit of a clown, wasn't he?'

Stephanie lifted an eyebrow. 'Really? You think so? I've seen ice cream melt slower than you did. I was just about to open his packet of cleaning sponges and wipe you off the patio.'

Edith felt her cheeks redden. They felt hot against the cool afternoon breeze. 'I don't know what came over me. He was quite a looker, wasn't he?'

'If you like people like that.'

'I mean, he came across as a spoilt rich kid, but—'

'You said it.'

Edith shook her head. The sun was beginning to drop

into the trees. They had probably half an hour of decent daylight left. Over to the west, grey clouds were starting to move in, threatening rain. Even as she looked up, a few spots pattered on the leaf litter around them.

'I think we should get inside,' she said. 'Finish getting our rooms sorted out.'

'Good idea.'

12

RAISING HELL

Any hopes of getting out for a nightcap were dashed when the rain began. What had looked like a passing shower turned out to be a major storm, and they cowered inside while wind and rain lashed the manor all evening. While the building had obviously been built to stand the test of time, certain parts of it seemed to be crying out in protest, with any attempts at a good night's sleep dashed by a relentless cacophony of creaking, rattling, whistling and shaking. After playing cards in the kitchen until nearly midnight, they both retired to bed, only to find themselves meeting in the hall less than half an hour later, both unable to sleep and spooked by the constant noise. In the end, they carried their bedding downstairs to the kitchen, where, despite a whistling from the chimney, the noise was mostly negated by its close proximity to the ground. They attempted to sleep again, both nodding off late into the night having spent much of their time chatting easily about anything and everything. Edith had revealed her rather embarrassing early teenage years' obsession with Ant from Ant and Dec, while

Stephanie was addicted to watching reruns of *Thundercats* on YouTube. Edith admitted to being haunted by a potentially winning goal miss in the final of the Devon Under 14s school netball final, and had never picked up a ball again. Stephanie confessed to having had a purple security blanket called Richie, the name of which had come from her father complaining 'Itchy, itchy!' when a requirement of hugging an infant Stephanie was that he had to hug the blanket as well.

While the wind had abated by morning, the rain was unrelenting, so with no way to get outside without getting drenched, they continued to work through the house, piling boxes marked as junk into the entrance hall for later removal, uncovering long-buried furniture, vacuuming, dusting, wiping, tidying and sorting. Both were convinced they were saving Arnold Pickles a fortune by doing the work of several people, much of which—including a successful attempt to unblock a sink on the second floor by unscrewing the U-bend—required specialist attention. However, as the hours, and then the days began to tick by, they started to enjoy not only the freedom to go where they wanted in such a massive, sprawling house, but the challenge of testing their skills.

When Stephanie announced that she had spotted what looked like a hatch leading into a possible loft space, they played 'rock, scissors, paper' to see who would go up first. In the end, Edith held the ladder while Stephanie went up, only to discover that it wasn't a loft space at all, but an entirely new and secret floor, with no other access that they had yet discovered. Armed with a pair of torches and a broom to ward off the abundant spiderwebs, they crept along the only corridor low and narrow enough to make them feel bigger than children, until they came to a metal-framed door at the far end. Unlocked, it led out onto a hidden roof patio, concealed from the ground by the surrounding spires.

Clearly unused for some years, a couple of hardy, stubborn bushes had grown up out of an accumulation of leaf litter. On one side was an ancient telescope, rusted solid, its lens gummed up with dirt and its eyepiece missing, the small space stuffed with the ancient remains of a bird's nest. In the other was a set of wooden picnic furniture, so badly rotted that it collapsed at a single touch. From here, though, the grey thunderclouds overhead felt almost close enough to touch, and the views stretched over the surrounding trees towards distant hills.

'Which way is south?' Stephanie asked.

'Behind us, I think.'

'You might be able to see the church in Willow River if you climb up that spire a bit,' Stephanie said, pointing to a moss-laden slate roof that rose close enough to vertical to make climbing it impossible without specialist equipment or a foolhardy amount of bravery.

'I'll just take your word for it,' Edith said, momentarily concerned Stephanie meant to try the ascent, before catching that now-familiar little smile. 'Although this would make a great place for a glass of wine or two.'

'I wonder what's through there?' Stephanie said, pointing to another door on the other side. This one was locked, however, and while they were discussing trying to joggle the lock with a piece of metal drainpipe frame, it began to rain again. The surrounding spires shuddered and creaked as the wind gusted, and they hurried back inside before they could be blown away.

In a dusty cupboard in the corner of the entrance hall, they had found a stack of ancient board games. They got stuck into a tattered and faded Monopoly game, in which pieces shaped like a lantern and a cannon dated it to prewar, according to Stephanie, who turned out to be a board game nerd. However, after the first time she began to gesture like a chicken, Edith took over bank duties and the game was hard fought, Stephanie eventually coming out the winner with a narrow margin.

Nearly midnight by this time with the storm still raging outside, Edith suggested they go for a 'ghost walk' into the cellar, an entrance to which they had found near the back door into the kitchen.

'Only if you go first,' Stephanie said. 'I've had enough of spiderwebs. Any more and I'll start turning into Miss Havisham. Although I'd need a wedding dress.'

'Who?'

'From *Great Expectations*.' Stephanie shrugged. 'They had it in the prison library. Not a lot of choice in those places.'

'Prison? I didn't realise you'd actually done time.'

Stephanie shrugged. 'I was volunteering. Trying to change my ways.' She sighed. 'It didn't work.'

'How about if I lock you in the cellar?'

'I'll be sure to haunt you for all eternity.'

'Thanks. Just be quiet at night.'

The cellar was dank and dark, their torch beams illuminating what at first looked like shelves hung with bedsheets as holey as string vests. A few steps closer revealed that in fact they weren't bedsheets at all, but thick crusts of ancient spiderwebs hung with decades old dust.

'Okay, time for bed,' Stephanie said, starting to go back up the stairs, but Edith grabbed Stephanie's sleeve.

'Wait!' she said. 'Look what's back there.'

Stephanie had clearly lost interest in any kind of midnight adventure, so waited on the stairs while Edith went down to the bottom to investigate what was hidden behind the curtain of ancient filth. Nudging a little aside with her torch, she revealed what she had thought she had seen, and smiled.

'Wine racks,' she said. 'Dozens of them.'

Moving aside enough of the crusty curtain to pull one free, she wiped dust off the label and read the inscription.

'It's some 1937 vintage from some squiggly place in Bordeaux,' she said. 'I can't read the town name. It's too faded.'

'Is it even safe to drink at that age?' Stephanie asked.

Edith grinned. 'Only one way to find out.'

'Well, grab one and bring it up. I don't think we should be drinking Lord Pickles's wine, though.'

'He expressly said that anything not labelled to be kept or thrown away was ours to do with as we wished.'

'I know, but even so.'

'Says you with the criminal record.'

Stephanie's face dropped. Edith felt a pang of regret.

'Look, I'm sorry; I didn't mean it like that. I'm just excited, that's all. This stuff is like buried treasure.'

'I know. It's all right. It can't hurt to have a look.'

Edith swung the torch around, inspecting the other racks. 'Oh, what do we have over here?'

A corner shelf held a number of bottles standing upright. Edith didn't have to look too closely to know these were spirits, and from the look of them, extremely old. She picked one at random and carried it back to Stephanie.

'Check this out. Louis the Twelfth brandy. Isn't that ridiculously expensive?'

'You're thinking of Louis the Thirteenth.'

'Well, wouldn't this be even older? It's probably worth a fortune.' She looked up at Stephanie, heart thundering with excitement. 'Shall we have a little sip? We can always top it up and put the top back on. Lord Pickles will never know.'

'I'm not sure.'

Edith, though, perhaps stirred by the storm, couldn't resist. She carried the bottle up to the kitchen, dusted it off and set it down on the table. Then she took two glasses from the cupboard. Stephanie watched her as she picked up the bottle, which surprisingly had a screw cap. She unscrewed it, poured a tiny amount into each glass, then looked up at Stephanie.

'It's only a little bit.'

'You go first.'

Edith grinned and lifted the glass. 'Okay. Here we go—'

The brandy had barely touched her lips when an almighty crack of thunder came from outside. The window lit up, and Edith jumped, spilling the rest of the brandy down the front of her top. The lights flickered and went off, leaving a small fire flickering through the glass door of the range as the only light in the room. Another flash came from outside, followed by a long, low groaning sound.

'Get back!' Stephanie shouted, jumping up and rushing towards Edith. She scooped her up out of her seat, throwing her over her shoulder and running for the door just as the window exploded behind them and the kitchen filled with wet, swaying branches, the last of the season's leaves scattering across the floor.

'Wow,' Stephanie said, a shadowy flicker on her face as she put Edith down.

'What happened?' Edith gasped, even as the tree branches shuddered and shook, and rain lashed through the broken window. The fire, caught in a gust of wind, flickered and went out, leaving them in near total darkness.

'I don't think you should have drunk that brandy,' Stephanie said. 'You've made Fieldy angry.'

13

CUTTING CREW

While not quite encapsulating the dramatics of the actual event, the towering maple tree, struck by lightning during the storm, had made a significant mess of the kitchen window and its surrounds. With a warm autumn sun beaming out of a clear, almost mocking sky, they surveyed the damage by the not-so-cold light of day.

It quickly became clear both how lucky they had been not to be hurt, and also how they would need specialist help in order to shift the fallen tree. While Stephanie could just about touch her fingertips around its trunk, Edith was several inches short, and while they could probably hack off a few of the side branches, they needed proper equipment to cut and remove the trunk before they could even think about repairing the window.

'Do you think we should call Lord Pickles?' Stephanie asked as they stood on the embankment outside the rear kitchen, the fallen tree beside them, the remains of the splintered trunk pointing skyward, scorch marks across the wood. The tree had stood some way off from the house;

that its upper branches now filled half of the kitchen was testament to how massive it had been.

'I don't think he'll be too happy about it,' Edith said. 'I mean, I got the impression he's taking us for a bit of a ride, but even so, he might fire us anyway. And then we're both out of a job. I know it's not much, but I really need the money. We have to get that tree out and that window fixed before he or his grandson shows up.'

'And James is due to come by and pay us tomorrow, isn't he?'

'Right.' Edith frowned, then clicked her fingers. 'Didn't you say there was a timber merchant just up the road? Where you … borrowed that chainsaw?'

'I don't think they'll be happy to see me around.'

'But didn't you say you put it back without anyone noticing?'

'Well, yeah, but what if someone did?'

'Look, we don't have a lot of choice. If you want, I'll go.'

'No, we'll both go. I can face up to my crimes. Even if it was you that drank the brandy that set Fieldy's wrath upon us.'

Edith glanced at Stephanie, but the other girl was grinning. 'It wasn't worth it,' she said. 'It tasted like every other time I've tried brandy. Horrible. We'll put it back once we've cleared enough of the tree to get back into the cellar.'

Stephanie sighed. 'All right, let's go.'

'The worst they can do is say no.'

'No, the worst would be "We saw you on our CCTV stealing a chainsaw, and the police are on their way."' She let out a low growl and clenched a fist. 'I'm ready to face my punishment.'

'You'll be fine. If they mention it, tell them you wanted to try-before-you-buy. Just don't steal any more.'

'I'll try not to.'

'Remember the chicken thing? As soon as you get the urge.'

'Got it.'

They headed up Maple Tree Lane to the timber merchant, which was down a narrow track near the junction onto the main Willow River to Brentwell Road. Set back from the road, they heard the sound of cutting equipment before the yard had even come into sight. Stephanie looked nervous and ready to flee for the road, but as they turned the corner to see a series of works buildings and stacks of logged trees in front of them, a dachshund came bobbing out of a kennel by the roadside, berating them with a hoarse yap.

'What a darling,' Stephanie said, squatting down and patting her knees as the dog bumbled closer. 'I always wanted a sausage dog.'

The dog gave her a huffed growl, then relented and wandered over to sniff her hand. A moment later, it was lying on its back while she rubbed its tummy.

'Some guard dog,' Edith muttered.

'You all right over there?' came a crusty old voice above the sound of the chainsaws. The door to a cabin office had opened and an old man was limping across the yard, leaning on a stick, one leg dragging behind the other. 'Help you girls? Looking for a new kitchen table?' He grinned, most of his teeth absent. 'Presentation gives your cooking skills a boost, eh?'

Edith lifted an eyebrow. 'Just use a higher setting on the microwave,' she said.

'Ah, a modern girl.' The old man grinned. 'The name's Rick. What can I do you for?'

'We're staying up the road at Trenton Manor,' Edith said. 'We're doing some … work for Lord Pickles.'

'Ah, Pickles up at Hell House? Finally putting that old monstrosity to bed, is he? Bulldozer's round 'back. I can have him up there in twenty minutes.'

'Nothing quite so dramatic,' Edith said. 'We had a tree go down in the storm last night, and we need to get it removed before….'

She trailed off, shrugging.

'Before Lord Pickles finds out and fires us,' Stephanie finished, patting the dog, now sitting up, on its back, its tongue lolling with delight.

Rick nodded. 'Ah, got you's. You'll need my boys with their chainsaws. Wait here while I give them a call. Watch that dog don't bite. Savage in her younger days, weren't you, Marge?'

The dog gave an affirmative little yap, then continued to pant as Stephanie rubbed its back.

Rick hobbled over to a shed, pulled open a corrugated-iron door with a forceful jerk that defied his fragile stature, and shouted inside. A moment later, the machines cut off. Rick turned and hobbled back to Edith and Stephanie. Just as he reached them, two men appeared. Both were broad and muscular through t-shirts stained with sweat, dirt and paint, although one towered over the other by at least six inches. While the shorter of the two had the physique of a middleweight boxer and the looks of a TV dating show contestant, the taller looked capable of uprooting trees with his hands.

'My boys,' Rick said with a hint of pride as the two men came up behind him and gave the girls awkward smiles, shifting from foot to foot as though either keen to get back to work or change into clothing more appropriate for meeting strangers. 'On the left is my grandson,

Anthony, and the giant on the right is my great nephew, Max.'

Edith stared at Anthony, alarm bells ringing. He met her stare, eyes slowly widening, followed by a smile on his strikingly handsome face.

'Edith ... Davies? Is that you? Wow. Talk about blast from the past. Don't think I've seen you since you pushed me into the school pond.'

Edith's cheeks reddened. 'Anthony Wallen? It's ... been a while, hasn't it? I had no idea you were still around.'

Antony spread his hands. 'Right here. Still traumatised. I got a bit of pondweed in my mouth. I can no longer go near water.' He grinned. 'Even rain frightens me.'

'I'm sorry about that ... I was only about eleven.'

'We were playing kiss chase; do you remember? You caught me by the side of the pond. I was a little chunkier then. I refused, so you pushed me in.'

A cackle of laughter came from Rick. Edith, cheeks burning, glanced at Stephanie, but her friend was staring, unblinking at Max, who was returning her stare open-mouthed. As Edith watched them, she could imagine some sort of bridge forming between them, beneath which Rick and Marge resembled rather ungainly sailing boats. Just as she smiled at this though, Stephanie tucked her arms up under her arms and began to cluck violently, turning in a circle bobbing her head up and down.

'What's going on with the lass?' Rick said, the connecting spell broken as Max and Anthony exchanged a bewildered glance. Edith grabbed Stephanie's arm and pulled her away from the group, grinning over her shoulder as she explained, 'My friend's having a bit of an episode. Hang on a moment.'

As soon as they were far enough away to avoid being

overhead, Edith leaned in close. 'What happened there? You wanted to steal something, didn't you?'

Stephanie looked at her, eyes filled with hopelessness as a tear ran down her cheek. 'Yes,' she said, almost sobbing. 'I did.'

'What on earth was there to steal?'

Stephanie sniffed. 'His heart.'

14

PAY DAY

'Well, that's made a quite a mess, hasn't it?' Anthony said, one foot up on the trunk of the fallen tree. 'I'd say Pickles should have had these trees cut back years ago, but he was rarely here. I don't think he had much interest in this place.'

'It must be nice to be so rich you can forget about a country mansion,' Edith said. 'I mean, if you polished it up a bit you could make it really pretty.'

'And that's what he's employing you and Stephanie to do?'

Edith shrugged. 'I'd just lost my job and my flat. Stephanie wasn't working. My dad bumped into Arnold Pickles and probably saw an opportunity.'

'He's getting a bit of a bargain, if you ask me. It's like Pickles to squeeze every drop out of someone, though. He's that kind of man. For years he's been hassling Granddad about the fence around our property. He claims it's six inches onto his land.' He smiled. 'That's only because he never cuts his hedges and the weeds are pulling our fence over. Granddad refuses to cut them back for him. Pickles even went so far as to send his grandson down to hassle us. He thought Granddad was on his own and started getting all bully boy on him. Didn't realise me and Max were out the back. We made it clear in no uncertain terms that he's not welcome on our property.'

'Do you mean James?'

'Yeah.'

'We met him. He brought us some cloths.'

'Careful he doesn't take the cost out of what pittance he's paying you. Don't be surprised if he sends you an invoice.'

'Are we liable for criminal damage for this tree?'

Anthony shook his head. 'Not at all. See how the roots are sticking out of the ground? It's been a fall risk for several years, I imagine. He should have had it cut back. Don't worry, we'll clear it out. Pretty sure Granddad knows someone who can do that window at a pinch too.' He planted big hands on his hips and looked around. 'I wonder where Max and Stephanie got to? Weren't they making coffee?'

'On a camping stove on the front patio,' Edith said.

'Does it really take that long to boil some water?'

Edith smiled. 'Maybe sometimes.'

They were still standing by the tree, assessing the damage when the sound of whistling announced the return of Stephanie and Max. While not quite arm in arm, they were walking close enough to each other that it was clear they had made some kind of connection. Max, whistling the *Thundercats* theme tune, held back a piece of protruding bramble for Stephanie to carry a tray with four steaming mugs up to the embankment, where she set it down on a section of stump which Anthony and Max had already chainsawed flat.

'Coffee time,' she said in a cheerful voice, then looked at Max and flashed a wide grin.

Edith glanced at Anthony, who shrugged.

After their break was over, they got to work; Anthony and Max cleaning off the side branches and then cutting through the trunk and rolling the pieces away. Edith and Stephanie were charged with hauling the cut branches up to a corner of the garden where they could be piled for chopping up later. It was a hard afternoon's work, but by the time Rick's glazier friend, Johnny Dent, showed up at just after four o'clock, they had cleared the tree away and picked up all the broken glass. Johnny, giving a knowing nod at the mention of Arnold Pickles, got straight to work, and by six o'clock they had a new window. Replaced curtains hid the building work from the inside, and while Pickles might notice if he took a wander around the back of the house, if the current neglected state of the house was anything to go by, he probably wouldn't notice at all.

After Johnny had left, Edith and Stephanie shared another coffee and a slice of cake with Anthony and Max, then bid the two men goodnight. Almost as soon as the entrance door had closed, Stephanie began hyperventilating.

'Oh my God, oh my God, oh Fieldy! Do you think he likes me?'

Edith smiled. 'You took your time making the coffee.'

Stephanie shrugged. 'We were looking at the rose bushes by the patio and Max told me he liked to grow them in his free time. He said he would name the next hybrid he made after me. The Stephanie Rose. Can you believe it?'

'I think I'm going to be sick.'

'He said there's probably already one called that, but ours will be a special one. He wants to take me to the cinema in Brentwell this weekend. Do you think he likes me?'

'His mother was probably busy.'

'Really? You think so?'

'No. He clearly likes you. Just go with the flow.' She patted Stephanie on the arm. 'And don't steal anything.'

Stephanie smiled. 'I already told Max about that. He said he understood. But do you know what? I don't feel like stealing anything anymore. It's like I found what I wanted.'

'Good for you. I hope it works out.'

Stephanie grinned. 'What about you and Anthony?'

'What about us? I pushed him in the school pond. I don't think he likes me all that much.'

'I saw him looking at you.'

'Don't be silly. We were just talking about the tree.'

Stephanie patted Edith on the shoulder this time, hard enough to make Edith stagger. 'If you say so.'

∼

Friday was another fine day, but Edith's body was screaming after an afternoon of hauling wood. As she hobbled into their newly restored kitchen, she found Stephanie sitting at the table, two coffees already made and a slice of blueberry-topped cheesecake next to Edith's cup.

'Max stopped round while you were still in bed,' Stephanie said, beaming. 'He brought this cheesecake he said we really had to try. Did you know his mother owns the cake shop on Brentwell High Street?'

'I do now,' Edith said. 'It's only half past seven. He must have got up early.'

'He was on his way to work. I'm going to meet him for lunch over at the timber merchant. You … don't mind, do you?'

Edith smiled. 'No, that's fine. I hope you have a good time.'

Even as she said it though, she felt a pang of advance loneliness. She hadn't realised just how much she had come to like Stephanie until faced with the possibility of losing her friend. That Stephanie was almost deliriously happy was scant consolation; Edith couldn't help but feel a pang of jealousy towards Max. Still, it would only be for lunch. And afterwards they could do the girly thing and discuss everything Max had said. It felt almost sisterly in a way, something Edith had missed out on after Ellen had run off to America before Edith had begun to show any interest in boys.

Both aching from the previous day's endeavours, they took things a little easier in the morning, concentrating on a bit of simple cleaning on the ground floor. Behind the piles of boxes and under some of the dusty sheets they encountered numerous curios and fascinating artefacts, including a stuffed replica dodo which they had swiftly covered back up, and a full-sized snooker table. Stopping to have a quick game, Stephanie had muttered something about being a member of Brentwell Juniors, before sinking a table-length red and then promptly racking up a break of thirty-five while Edith was still figuring out how to hold the cue. Stephanie, apologising for an obviously high-amateur level of skill after each potted ball, quickly finished Edith off, then offered to teach her a few basics. Edith just smiled and told her it was probably time for another coffee.

Shortly after uncovering a suit of armour which Stephanie was trying to encourage Edith to try on, the doorbell gave a sharp ring. Quickly hiding the half-disassembled suit under a sheet, they headed for the front door, where they found James Archer-Pickles waiting for them.

'Good morning, ladies,' he greeted them with a bright smile as they let him in, where he set down a hold-all bag on the floor. 'I come bearing gifts, girls,' he said, looking up at them with a smile on his hopelessly handsome face. 'Look. I have a pack of disposable rubber gloves—extra large for Steph, but Edie, you can probably wear two pairs.'

'No worries, *Jay*,' Edith said.

'More scrubbing brushes, some replacement hoover bags, some drain cleaner....' He looked up at them, still grinning, and clapped his hands together. 'It must be like Christmas.'

'Thanks,' Edith said.

'Drum roll, please.' James shook his hands up and down, grinning from ear to ear. 'And here ... are your pay envelopes.' He winked. 'Used notes of course.'

'Thanks.' Edith attempted to smile as she opened the stuffed envelope. It was notes as he had said, all wrinkled five-pound notes as though he'd been rummaging down the back of a couple of hundred used sofas and used his loot to pay them. As she counted them, though, it became clear there was a discrepancy.

'There doesn't seem to be much here,' she said.

'Ah, Dad had to take a few deductions,' James said. 'It's all on that note inside.'

Edith pulled out a crumpled piece of paper and attempted to read the scrawled handwriting. 'Temporary tax, National Insurance, key money? What?'

'It's a deposit to ensure the house keys are returned when you're finished.'

Edith rolled her eyes, then continued down the list. 'Room and board ... utilities? Are you serious?'

'It's a token deduction,' James said. He leaned forward and pointed at the last line. 'Look there.'

'Accrued bonus seventy-five pounds.'

'That's more like it, isn't it?'

'But where is it?'

'Oh, you get it at the end, when you're done. Should be quite a bit of Christmas money by then, shouldn't it?'

Edith could only glare at him. Stephanie, seemingly unconcerned, kept looking up at the grandfather clock in the hall.

'Well, thanks,' Edith said at last.

'No problem. Grandfather sends his best,' James said, turning to the door. 'Well, as best he can. I think he's on the way out, but he's a stubborn old so-and-so. Have you ever been in a Bugatti? Beautiful cars. I saw this Chiron I want to put on order, but I have to wait until the deal's done first.'

'The house sale?' Edith asked, trying to sound interested.

'No. Grandfather's passing.'

'Oh.'

'Obviously I don't want him to die, but since he's going to, no point in drawing it out, is there?'

Edith just stared at him as he lifted his hand to wave, then jogged back down the driveway.

'He's ... callous,' she said.

'Do you mind?' Stephanie said, shifting from foot to foot. I'm going to be late for Max.'

'Go,' Edith pressed. 'Don't worry, I'll be fine. I'll make a voodoo doll of James out of some old cushions or something.'

'Thanks so much,' Stephanie said, pulling on her shoes so quickly she nearly toppled over. 'See you later?'

'Have a good time. Don't rush back. I'll be all right.'

Edith watched as Stephanie raced down the driveway. She looked deliriously happy, at one point appearing to do a Mary Poppins-esque skip, before Edith realised she had caught her foot on a root and narrowly avoided ploughing into a hedge. And then she was out of sight, and Edith was left standing on the porch of the crumbling old manor house, all alone.

'All right, Fieldy,' she said to the overgrown garden, giving a long sigh. 'Just me and you now.'

She went back through the house, down the long corridor and the stone steps to the kitchen, which she had begun to treat as her favourite hangout space, now that the window had been repaired. Rick had lent them a kettle and a microwave so she made another coffee and sat at the long trestle table, staring at where Stephanie had usually sat, feeling an acute sense of loneliness without her friend. She remembered the resentment she had felt at finding Stephanie lodging at her parents' place, but Stephanie's absence wasn't just accentuated by her huge frame, but by the warmth of her personality, and without it, the house felt cold and dead.

She finished her coffee, then wondered about lunch. The clock in the hall, that with a bit of jostling and poking around they had managed to restart, had just chimed twelve. Edith suddenly didn't want to be alone in this old house. She got up, glaring at her pay packet as she stuffed it into her pocket. For the work they had done, it was a pittance, but it would at least buy her lunch.

She was just about to put on her shoes when she remembered they hadn't yet returned the postcards Stephanie had stolen from the shop. Thinking Stephanie wouldn't mind, and that it might be easier to explain the situation without Stephanie present, Edith headed upstairs to get them. Stephanie's door was ajar and Edith spotted the postcards in a neat pile on a table by the window.

They looked just like they had when Stephanie had

taken them from the shop. Edith paused, feeling a little intrusive, but surely Stephanie wouldn't mind. She went inside and took them off the tabletop. As she turned back to the door, however, she saw something poking out from under Stephanie's pillow.

It looked like another postcard, but this one had a foreign stamp visible on the protruding corner. Edith stared at it, hating her curiosity, but then remembered how Stephanie had appeared to have fallen asleep with it in her hand. She went over to the bed and lifted up the corner of the pillow just enough to see the postcard beneath.

The stamp was unknown to her, but the postcard was obviously old and well-thumbed. A barely readable line of typed text along the top said *Catedral de Cordoba, Cordoba, Argentina*. The edges of the postcard had been touched so many times that they were almost worn away, but the inscription in black ink was still readable:

Dear Stephanie,
I am starting to get back on my feet again. I'm so sorry for everything. I made a lot of mistakes and I hope you can forgive me. Once I get myself together, I hope perhaps you can come and visit me for a while. I'll be in touch again once I have a permanent address.
Love always,
Dad

Edith wiped a tear off her cheek, then gently laid the pillow back down. Then, with her heart gently breaking, she took the stolen postcards and headed out of the room.

15

MEETING THE LOCALS

THE SUN WAS BEAMING OUT OF AN ICY BLUE SKY, THE breeze just chilly enough to make itself noticeable as Edith walked down Maple Tree Lane into Trenton. Crimson, orange and gold leaves fluttered around her, the sun dappling the road as she walked beneath the trees. She was already feeling better as she reached the stream, pausing for a couple of minutes to watch the fish flitting over the stones as the sun through the trees left glittering patterns on the water. The shop was still open, so she steeled herself and headed inside. The old woman was behind the counter, head down, reading a newspaper. Edith muttered 'Hello,' as the bell over the door tinkled. The old woman didn't look up, so Edith headed straight for the postcard rack, but to her dismay, it had gone.

She already had the postcards out in her hand, and had no choice but to put them down on the dusty windowsill behind a rack of gardening seed sachets. As she turned back, she caught movement out of the corner of her eye, and looked up to see the old woman standing in the aisle, glaring at her.

'You all right up there?'

'Ah, yes, I was just … ah, looking for a postcard.'

'Sold out, we have.'

'But … there are some here, on the window ledge,' Edith said, holding up the postcards she had just put down.

The old woman hobbled closer. 'Oh?' She lifted up her glasses, squinting at Edith. She held out a hand, and Edith passed her little stack.

'These old buggers. Out of date, ain't they?' She poked a finger at the picture on the front. 'See? Ain't got Daniel's new extension, nor that footbridge they built up the valley there. Who's gonna want these?'

'I don't know,' Edith said, shrugging as the old woman turned over the stack and peered at the bottom postcard.

'Dear Mum, we're having a lovely time at Trenton Manor,' the old woman read, as Edith's blood ran cold. 'Edith seems all right, although I think she has some family issues. I'll do what I can to help her. The house is nice, but a bit cold at night. Love, Stephanie.'

The old woman looked up. Edith wished she had a towel to wipe the sweat off her face.

'Ah—'

The old woman thrust the postcards at Edith's hand. 'Must be some factory misprint,' she said. 'Ain't no one up at Trenton Manor. Pickles, that old trout, he don't go up there much no more. Place been as good as abandoned for donkey's years. You got any draughty windows, you might find a use for these, otherwise just chuck them in the bin.'

'Sure,' Edith said.

'You pop back in a couple of days,' the old woman said. 'I'll get more on order. How many you after?'

'Um … just one.'

The old woman grinned. 'Boyfriend?'

'Ah, no. My … sister?'

'Huh. My old sister wouldn't spit on me if I were dead,' the old woman said. 'Well, can't, because she's already dead.'

Edith didn't know what to say. After a few seconds of laughing nervously along to the old woman's witchlike cackle, she waved a hand and backed out of the shop, the fresh breeze immediately chilling the sweat on her brow. She wiped her face with her sleeve and headed for the pub.

It was a little too cold to sit outside, and on her own she preferred the inconspicuousness of an indoor table anyway. The landlord gave her a kind smile, asked after Stephanie and then introduced himself as Matt Compton.

'You're seeing Trenton in the best season,' he told her as she ordered a coffee and a Ploughman's. 'Well, if you excuse the storm earlier in the week. We've got another week of the leaves, I think. You going to come to the harvest festival next weekend? It's at the village hall, which you'll find if you take the lane across the street there which leads up along the river.' Matt gave a sudden sigh. 'I remember when we used to hold it in the grounds of Trenton Manor. Colin and Amelia really loved that place.'

'Who?'

'Arnold Pickles's son and his wife. They were the last lord and lady of the manor, so to speak.'

'What happened to them?'

Matt sighed. 'They were on safari in Kenya. Colin was a nice guy, but not the brightest firework on Guy Fawkes Night, if you get what I mean. He was a keen amateur photographer and wanted a close-up of a pride of lions on a safari trip. He'd just got some sponsorship deal with an up-and-coming camera manufacturer, and was getting more and more adventurous with his photographs. He did the one thing you're never supposed to do, and got out of the car.'

'Oh. He got eaten by lions?'

Matt grimaced. 'Not all of him. I think they got some bits back.'

'Ouch. His wife must have been heartbroken.'

'Yeah, kind of. Apparently, she found comfort with one of the tour guides, and ended up getting married again a few months later. I heard she died a few years later at an elephant sanctuary when a misfiring car engine caused a group of recently rescued elephants to stampede.'

'That's quite a pair of tragedies.'

Matt grinned. 'The kind only rich old people seem to suffer. Give me a heart attack in the vegetable garden any day.'

'After they left, Arnold had no interest in the house?'

'Not really. He popped down from time to time to make sure there were no squatters, I suppose. He has his properties in London, up where there's a bit of action. And James, the heir to all of it, is a chip off his grandfather's block. Content to just burn through the family fortune as quickly as he can. Arnold just fired all the staff, left the house empty. That was probably twenty years ago.'

'Me and my friends used to dare each other to sneak into the grounds,' Edith said. 'Back when we were teenagers. We were always too scared to try to get into the house itself, though.'

'Rumour has it that it's got all sorts of secrets,' Matt said. 'The biggest one of course is that Julius Pickles, Arnold's great-grandfather, won it in a gambling game from another local landowner, Marcus Mansfield.' Matt's eyes twinkled. 'Part of local folklore, that story. Ask old Barbara in the shop if you're interested. Her family have been in Trenton since the dinosaurs died out.' He winked. 'There are people that say they evolved from them directly, and that Barbara herself is a direct descendant from the tyrannosaurus rex.'

'She's not that scary.'

'Oh, she was in her day. She used to lead all the local scout groups, and she led them like a military commander. We won all sorts of competitions for orienteering and survival, river rafting, you name it. But for each of those dusty trophies in the cabinets up in the village hall, there's a little piece of human soul.' He leaned over the bar, lowering his voice. 'Plus, next time you're in there, see how short her arms are in comparison to her body.' He tapped the side of his face. 'T-Rex, I'm telling you, and most people round here will say the same.' He looked up at the clock and grimaced. 'And … anyway, I was getting your food order, wasn't I?'

Edith grabbed a magazine out of a rack by the door and took it to a corner table. She tried to read but couldn't concentrate on anything at all, her thoughts consumed with all the mad theories Matt had filled her head with. All pretty fanciful, but fun, nonetheless. Taking on the cleaning job at Trenton Manor had certainly been an adventure so far.

When Matt brought over her food a few minutes later, she said, 'I don't suppose you're hiring bar staff? Once I'm finished at Trenton Manor, I'll be unemployed.'

Matt chuckled. 'I'm afraid what you see is a typical day at this time of year. I might have a few hours over Christmas and New Year, but we don't get the customers down here these days. Certainly not enough to hire more full-time staff. We get a handful in for lunch, but nothing I can't handle on my own.'

'Not to worry. If you hear of anything, please let me know. I'll probably stop in from time to time.'

'Sure, will do. What happened to your friend, by the way?'

Edith grinned. 'She's got a date, with Max from up at the timber merchant.'

'Max? You mean Annie and Kevin Wallen's boy? Lovely chap. Size of a house, personality to match. Mind you, she's a big lass, your friend, isn't she?'

Edith smiled. 'I hope they get on okay. She's not had it easy.'

'None of us have. I don't get the impression you've had it smooth, either. No one ends up working for Arnold Pickles and his padlocked wallet by choice.'

'Yeah, the pay's not the best.'

'Oh, well here could be your chance to ask for a pay rise.' Matt was staring out of the window. Edith turned, just in time to see a sleek sports car pull into the pub car park.

'Is that James?'

'Yeah. Right, time to be the good landlord. If he annoys you, just give me a shout.'

Matt went back behind the bar, and a moment later the door opened and James marched in. He looked expensive, everything from his shoes to his haircut, like he'd stepped out of a shop window in Mayfair. He was easy on the eye too, handsome in a manicured, honed way, his body tight beneath the suit, every part of him scrubbed, trimmed, filed and gelled.

'Barkeep,' he greeted Matt, who gave him a professional smile. 'Am I too late for a spot of local grub?'

Matt's smile never wavered. 'What would you like?'

'I'll have one of those spiral sausage things,' James said.

'Cumberland sausage?'

'Yeah, that'll do. And a pint of lager.'

'Aren't you driving?'

'Yeah, but not far. I'm staying just up the road. A little place on the way to Willow River.'

'All right. I can only serve you the one, though.'

James sighed. 'All right, if you're making moral choices for people, just make it a half.'

'You wouldn't want to scratch such a fine motor,' Matt said, pouring the drink and handing it across. 'What is it, a Porsche? We don't see many of those around here.'

'I own the manor house up the road,' James said.

'Ah, I thought I recognised you. James Pickles, isn't it?'

'James *Archer*-Pickles.'

'Twang,' Matt said, lifting his hands and making a surreptitious bow-and-arrow gesture while James was staring at the beer pumps.

'What?'

'Just come by to cut the grass?'

'Oh God no. I'm staying locally. We have people in, tiding the place up so we can put the old barn on the market. Not much reason to live round here, but you can usually fool a rich retiree from London, can't you?' He chuckled.

'Do you want to pay now, or later?'

'Might as well get it out of the way.' James held up a credit card. 'I'll have locals' prices, of course.'

'Sure. With the Cumberland sausage, that's nineteen-pounds fifty.'

'What? Are you serious?'

Matt grinned. 'Locals' price. All the locals round here are loaded.'

Edith was unable to suppress a laugh. James turned at the sound, noticing her for the first time. 'Oh, Edie, didn't see you over there. Lunch break, is it?'

Edith nodded. 'Yes.'

'We must be paying you too much.' Then, turning back

to Matt, James said, 'Barkeep, I'll eat over there, with the lady.'

'If that's okay with her,' Matt said, his smile dropping. Edith just lifted a hand.

'It's okay,' she said.

James brought over his half a lager and sat down. As soon as he did so, he nodded at Edith's drink and lifted an eyebrow.

'Does my grandfather know that you're drinking on the job?'

'It's coffee.'

James looked momentarily put out, then gave a little shudder as though to compose himself. 'Is that what they call it these days?'

'As far as I know,' Edith said with a tired sigh. 'I need enough fuel to get back up the hill.' Then, unable to resist, she smiled and added, 'You won't tell him, will you?'

James lifted an eyebrow again, bouncing it up and down, leaving Edith wondering if he had a trapped nerve or perhaps a tic. 'That depends on whether you let me buy you dinner. My calendar is full for the next week or so, but how about next Saturday?'

'Oh, I … don't know.'

'You can't be busy, otherwise you wouldn't be sitting here. I trust your friend is scrubbing away up there?'

'Of course.'

'Good. Rotating lunch breaks. That's the kind of work ethic my grandfather likes. Anyway, dinner. I'm prepared to pay, of course. I'm sure there's somewhere half-decent in Brentwell. I can pick you up. I'm staying pretty close, renting this little place up by the main road. A little cottage. A little cramped, but its comfortable enough.'

'That's my—'

'It's owned by Ellen Davies's parents. You know, the

famous screenwriter. She's done some great stuff. Have you seen *Transcendent*? It was fantastic.'

Edith shook her head. 'No, I haven't seen it.'

'You know, you look a fair bit like her. Kind of like a less glossy version.'

'That's because she's my sister.'

James's eyes widened. 'Is that right? Huh, what a coincidence.'

Edith forced a smile. 'Yes, amazing, isn't it?'

'She's a screenwriter; you're cleaning houses. Sounds like you missed the boat somewhere, didn't you?'

'Fell right in.'

'You don't happen to have a key to her room, do you?'

'Nope. My dad is preserving it.'

'It must be great being related to someone famous,' James said. 'Don't worry, if you're seen out with me it'll raise your status a bit. You can take a picture for your Instagram.'

'I don't have an Instagram.'

'Make sure you wear something nice.'

'Have you ever worn half a Ploughman's salad?'

Just before she could upend what was left of her lunch over James's suit, Matt appeared with James's food. Edith nudged the table with her foot, wondering if she could turn the whole thing over, perhaps crushing James underneath, but it was pretty solid. Maybe Stephanie could do it, but Edith didn't have the power in her shoulders. Instead, she stuffed a last piece of cheese into her mouth and stood up.

'Sorry to run,' she mumbled, 'But I've got to get back to scrubbing your house's crusty old toilets.'

'We're on for next Saturday, then?' James said. 'I'll remind you next week when I stop by with your pay.'

'Only if you call me Ellen all night.'

James grinned. 'It's a deal.'

Matt gave her a wave farewell as she headed for the door, but she needed the walk up the hill to work off her frustration. How could such entitled people exist in the world, acting like the sun orbited around them? And how —unfortunate demise of parents notwithstanding—could they land on their feet with such consummate ease?

She paused at a gate to look down across a field towards the valley. Sheep chewed nonchalantly on grass without a care in the world. A stream threaded its way through trees, glittering beneath the last golden leaves of autumn. Edith squeezed her eyes shut, opening them again to find everything was much the same. It would all go on without her, without any of them. The sheep would chew grass for all eternity.

Screw it. She would go on the date with James. So what if he called her Ellen all night, considered her a second-rate, less attractive version of her famous sister? He was richer than the Duchy of Cornwall by the look of things. Perhaps she could marry him, then divorce him after a month and get Trenton Hall in the settlement? Maybe she could wear her wedding dress and haunt the corridors of Hell House for the rest of her days.

By the time she got back to the house, she felt even worse, the delightful scenery along Maple Tree Lane doing nothing to help her mood.

The tinkling of a piano was audible from outside. Edith frowned, approaching the front entrance. Was that Stephanie? It was hard to tell what was being played through the barrier of the door, but as Edith let herself inside, she blinked in surprise.

Stephanie was playing some kind of jazz piece, the notes fluid and soulful, rising high into the rafters of the house. Edith crept along the corridor to what they had dubbed the music room, and saw Stephanie from behind, sitting at the piano, hands moving gracefully over the keys.

And as she watched, Stephanie leaned back and begun to sing in a deep, sanguine voice, perfectly pitched, powerful enough to fill the room with its elegant beauty.

Edith, stunned, amazed, astounded, floored by her friend's remarkable talent, only felt more worthless than ever.

16

CONFRONTATION

'You told me you could play a bit,' Edith said. 'Those were your actual words. "I can play a bit." Like, you're actually a female Elton John.'

Stephanie, looking at her hands, blushed. 'That's nice of you to say. My dad said I sounded like Norah Jones.' She sniffed, wiping away a tear, and Edith remembered the postcard she had seen.

'You're better than Norah Jones. You should do a concert tour and have her support you.'

'I can't play in front of people. I would have stopped if I'd known you were there. My dad used to take me to lessons when I was a little girl. I only ever liked playing for him. One of the helpers at the hostel used to teach me after Mum and me moved in there, but I only played what she told me to play. I used to break into the local school at night to practise on a keyboard with headphones on.'

Edith smiled. 'You must have been the only kid in the world to break into a school in order to do more work. That's against the natural order of things.'

'It wasn't really work. I got an E on my music GCSE

because I was scared of being found out. On my music test, I played *Twinkle, Twinkle, Little Star*, and fluffed a couple of notes just for effect.'

'That's … self-destructive.'

Stephanie sniffed. 'I can't help it.' She shook her head. 'I feel like with everything I do, I'm trying to break myself.'

Edith sighed. 'At least you're doing something. I feel like I'm slowly dissolving, but in a really passive, unnoticeable way. Like, if someone gave me a spade, I couldn't even dig a hole for myself. I'd just kind of scrape at the floor for a bit.'

'You did a good job of digging over those flowerbeds around the back of the house.'

'You think so?'

'Max told me he got bullied for his weight at school, and it just made him eat more. Then, he was out playing one day and a bunch of kids came along, threatened him. He climbed up a tree to get away, up really high, and he found he liked it. He said it made him feel strong.' Stephanie shrugged. 'So he took up rock climbing. It gave him confidence, not to mention muscles. The next time he got threatened, he stood his ground.'

'What happened?'

Stephanie smiled. 'They left him alone after that.'

'Good for him. Were you ever bullied for your weight or size?'

Stephanie shook her head. 'With the first kid that said anything, I got him in a headlock and shoved his face into some brambles at the bottom of the school playing field. No one said a word after that. Mind you, most people just ignored me, didn't speak to me at all.'

'Kids are cruel.'

'So are many adults.'

'So … now that I've found out your secret, can you tell me what you were playing?'

'Oh, I was just making something up. Just messing around with a few jazz chords.'

'What are jazz chords?'

'In basic terms, any chord with more than four different notes.' Stephanie turned back to the piano, laying her fingers over the keys. 'See this; this is an A chord: A note, C sharp note, E. Three notes. Then, if I add this one —' She played another key with her little finger, '—it becomes an A major suspended ninth.' She shrugged. 'Or something like that. I forget the names. Play a few like that together, though—' Her fingers flashed across the keys faster than Edith could follow, '—and you have jazz.'

'That's incredible.'

Stephanie shrugged. 'It's all right.'

Edith felt something growing inside her, like a wall of frustration she had to batter her way through. She squeezed her eyes shut, opening them again, seeing Stephanie sitting in front of her: huge, damaged, self-destructive, beautiful, talented beyond words.

She grabbed hold of Stephanie's arm. 'Listen.'

'Ouch, that hurts.'

'Just promise me something.'

'Okay….'

'Just … be you.'

'All right … I'll try.'

'Don't be a shadow. Don't hide behind some kind of mask. Let the world see you, and live with everything you have.'

'Are you drunk?'

Edith shook her head. 'Not yet, but I'm pretty tempted to go and poach a bottle out of the cellar.'

Keeping herself busy helped with the growing sense of loneliness, but it gnawed away at her like a rat nibbling on her toes while she slept. That Stephanie's happiness had gone beyond delirium to a state where her friend practically floated while she walked, while lovely to see, was like rubbing a little bit of chilli powder into the open wound of Edith's lacerated self-confidence. The higher Stephanie seemed to float, the lower Edith seemed to crawl.

The house, though, was a good distraction. They were always finding new rooms behind previously unnoticed doors, narrow service corridors, even a dusty, empty ballroom down a corridor they'd somehow overlooked for more than a week. And in each of those new spaces they found either junk that needed clearing or dirt and dust to wash and scrub away.

The gardens, too, were a beautiful enigma. Hacking their way through the jungle-like mass of grass, they discovered buried fountains, a bandstand, and a sculpture garden, surrounded by shrubs that had perhaps once been cut into animal shapes.

'That was definitely once a giraffe,' Stephanie said, pointing at one tall, narrow shrub that rose over their heads. 'It looks like it's got two heads now, though.'

'Perhaps we should chop one of them off,' Edith said. 'Have a go at fixing it.'

'Yeah, but which one? We might chop off the wrong one.'

In the end, they decided to leave the possible-giraffe alone and try their skills on a couple of other bushes instead. Armed with shears, they hacked and cut until they were done, then stood back to admire their handiwork.

'It's a mouse,' Edith said, pointing at an amorphous lump. 'That pointy bit is its nose, and that bit there is an ear.'

'It looks like a sponge,' Stephanie said. 'Mine's a horse.'

'It also looks like a sponge,' Edith said. 'I don't think we're too good at this, are we?'

'Why don't we invite Max and Anthony up to judge?'

Edith grimaced. 'I don't think I'd have a chance of winning. Max would obviously vote for you, and Anthony would vote for you because I pushed him in the school pond.'

'Oh, he's totally over that.'

'What do you mean?'

'We were talking about you. Anthony was saying how you've changed totally from school.'

Despite the cool air, Edith found herself tugging at the neck of her jumper. 'I have. So has he.'

Stephanie smiled. 'They got out some old school photos. You had a perm.'

Edith groaned. 'Seriously? I hoped no photos of that existed. It was Mum's idea. She got it into her head that an eighties revival was underway, and wanted me to be cutting edge. I looked like a pom-pom.'

'Anthony said you'd become cool.'

'Did he?' Edith's neck was starting to prickle with sweat. 'Well, that's nice. Anyway, I think we'd better get back, don't you?'

∼

The next day, Stephanie asked for a day off in order for Max to take her out. Edith agreed, but as soon as Stephanie had gone, the loneliness came in, wanting a party. Edith tried to concentrate by busying herself with cleaning, but wandering the gloomy corridors alone just made her feel more depressed than ever. In the end, she decided to go out for a walk. Instead of heading down to Trenton, however, she walked the opposite way, up Maple Tree Lane, past the timber merchant where Max and Anthony worked, towards her parents' place.

She wasn't trying to get a look at Anthony. Definitely not. She had no interest in him other than a passing one as a former classmate. They had nothing much in common that she could remember—he had been into rugby: she hated dirt; he had often been scolded for talking too much: she could count on one hand the number of times she had even raised a hand in class.

Even so, as she walked past the entrance to the timber merchant, she couldn't help but look down the lane, wondering if he might appear. From the road, however, you couldn't even see into the yard itself, so she was left disappointed.

Or was that relieved?

The timber merchant behind her, half a mile further on, through a stand of trees appeared the familiar slate roof of her parents' place. A pang of longing struck her dead in her tracks, and for a few seconds she could only stare at it, wishing things were different, stripping back the years perhaps to a time when everything was easier. At least, for her. The sweet spot, she thought, would have been around the age of eleven or twelve, when she was still oblivious to her parents' financial difficulties and Ellen had not yet run off. Puberty had not yet made her life a living hell, and school was just school; none of the drama that would come later.

With a smile she realised it would be around the time she had pushed Anthony into the school pond.

She was still lost in her memories when the howl of an

expensive car engine jogged her. A squeal of brakes was accompanied by a sudden burst of generic dance music, which itself was quickly shut off.

And then with a grimness like a dark, thunderstorm sky, she remembered.

James Archer-Pickles was renting her parents' place.

Feeling a little nosy—but not remotely resentful or jealous, of course—she walked on up the street until the car parked in her parents' driveway appeared through the trees.

James's Porsche, the same one she had seen outside the pub in Trenton.

She found herself walking quicker, reaching the bottom of the driveway just as James appeared out of the house, walked up to the car, and popped open the boot. Edith couldn't help moving a little closer as he re-emerged, carrying a plastic sheet in one hand and a heavy pair of bolt cutters in the other, still with a Wright's of Willow River price tag attached. As he turned back to the house, he noticed her.

'Oh, Ell—Edith, what a surprise.'

'James.'

'You're on your lunch break, are you?' He glanced at his watch. 'Yes, I suppose you'd still be okay to get back in time without any penalties. Do you want to grab a coffee? I've just got to put these things in my garage a moment.

'My....' Edith wrinkled her nose. 'It's not your garage. It's my parents'.'

'It's mine for the moment,' James said, then spread his arms, one sagging with the weight of the bolt cutters. 'All mine.'

'What are you doing with those?'

James looked at the bolt cutters as though he'd never seen them before.

Autumn on Maple Tree Lane

'Oh, these? Nothing much. I just had a little issue I need to deal with.'

'What issue? If you've got maintenance that needs doing, you probably need my dad's permission.'

'It's just a small thing.'

'What?'

James sighed and rolled his eyes. 'Well, if you must know, I dropped an important document in the hall, and at that moment a gust of wind came through the window, and blew it underneath your sister Ellen's door. Due to the nature of the document, I need to recover it.' He held up the bolt cutters. 'Don't worry, I'll replace your sister's door with a much better one. Your parents will understand.'

'No, you can't. My dad would never allow that. They keep Ellen's room like a shrine.'

'I promise not to touch anything.'

'If you do it, I won't go on a date with you.'

'Everything all right here?'

The voice by the driveway entrance made them both turn. Anthony stood there, dressed in work overalls. In his hand he held a supermarket shopping bag. Unshaven, his hair was a mess. Mud flecked his boots and work clothes.

'We're fine; run along,' James said.

Anthony lifted an eyebrow. 'Run along? Excuse me, mate, but I don't think it's up to you whether I walk on by or not.'

Edith, standing midway between them, squirmed like a worm on a fish hook. Anthony looked like he could handle himself in a fight, but James was the one holding a pair of bolt cutters.

'It's all right,' Edith said. 'Just a misunderstanding.'

Anthony looked at her. 'Are you sure? I can walk you back up to the house, if you like.'

James gave her a smug grin. 'Or I can drive you. Just in case it starts to rain.'

The sky was crystal blue, not even a wisp of cloud to be seen. The only blemish was a single aeroplane vapour trail passing across the sky to the north, the plane perhaps heading in the direction of Exeter airport.

'I'll be fine,' Edith said, wishing she could disappear.

James smiled again, so smugly he could have been stuffing a pair of chocolate muffins into his cheeks.

'Save your first time in a Porsche for our date on Saturday,' he said. 'Remember, seven o'clock? I'll pick you up outside the gate of *my* manor house.'

Edith couldn't look up at Anthony, who was lingering on her peripheral vision. She wanted to tell James to go to hell, but the words wouldn't come out.

'Well, if everything's all right, I'd better get back to work,' Anthony said, his tone a little crestfallen. 'Granddad's waiting for his lunch.'

'Don't keep Granddad waiting,' James said.

Anthony took a step, then paused, and for a moment Edith, only letting herself look at his feet, wondered if he would rush James, maybe picking him up and tossing him, caber-like, into the neighbouring field. Instead, without a word, he carried on up the road.

'Look, you have my apologies,' James said. 'I really can't condone these local do-gooders. They were the bane of my grandfather's life. You know, every single one of them wants something. Are we still on for next Saturday?'

Edith lifted a hand to her mouth and gave a little cough.

'I'm afraid I might be coming down with something,' she said. 'It's probably just the flu, although, with all the dust and damp in your grandfather's place, it could be the bubonic plague.'

17

FOLKLORE

Instead of going back to the house, Edith found herself walking in circles. She wandered the country lanes, eventually climbing over a stile which took her along a forest path and emerged by the bridge in Trenton. There, she found a bench and sat for a while, watching the last of the autumn leaves drifting down around her, feeling the chill of the November air on her skin.

The awkwardness of meeting James at her parents' place and then Anthony showing up felt like a cup of ice poured down her back. She wanted to shrug it all off as stupid and childish, but she couldn't help but feel uncomfortable, like she had missed an opportunity, perhaps. She had no interest in James and assumed their de facto date was now cancelled, but she had no interest in Anthony either. He was just some kid from school who had sat on the other side of class and with whom she had barely had any interaction, barring that one time when she had pushed him into the school pond.

Yet, even as she ran the highlights reel of the meeting through her mind, she couldn't help but let her thoughts linger on her old schoolmate. He had changed a lot. At school he had been loud and a little irritating, if she were honest about it. But then, were she to put a mirror in front of herself, wouldn't he have seen her as insular, stand-offish, maybe even a little stuck-up?

School was a polariser, but adulthood was in many ways a great leveller. So what if he worked in a timber merchant? She was currently a part-time cleaner. If they were going on statuses, he was at least a rung or two above, even if James, with his family fortune, was standing at the top, laughing, pouring oil over them as they tried to climb up.

No, James was—in her mother's words—kindly, a plonker; less kindly, a spoiled rich brat. Anthony was a hard-working man of the earth.

What on earth am I considering here?

She gave a little shudder, throwing off her thoughts. The river looked nice. Lots of pretty leaves floating on the surface. A fish or two. How wonderful.

Anthony—

'A penny for your thoughts, dear? Or, perhaps these days, a swipe of the credit card?'

At the voice coming seemingly out of nowhere, Edith nearly fell off the bench. She swung around, heart thundering, to find Barbara, the elderly shopkeeper, standing behind her, a basket in her gnarled old hands and a pointed hat perching on her head, shading her eyes, the sun catching on a nose that was a little too long to be safely human.

'Oh, I'm sorry, I didn't see you there,' Edith stammered, heart thundering, wondering if she had fallen asleep without realising and woken up in a Brothers Grimm fantasy.

The old woman held out the basket. Matt was right,

her arms did appear a little on the short side. 'Are you hungry, dear?'

Edith peered inside, terrified the basket would be full of red apples, but instead it was full of fat, spongy scones, each filled with cream and jam.

'Go on, dear, don't be shy. I'm just going to walk these up the road a little, see who's about the village. Past their best, but still perfectly okay with a little jam and cream.'

'Well, in that case, thanks. Don't mind if I do.'

As Edith reached into the basket, Barbara narrowed her eyes. 'Not up the spout, are you?'

'Excuse me?'

'Got one on the way?'

'Ah, no….'

'Must be just a little puppy fat, then,' Barbara said, leaning forward to give Edith a humiliating pat on the stomach. 'Not to worry, dear. Nothing that hill won't work off. Just stay off your sat-fats.'

'Ah, will do.'

'Every little one needs a bit of padding,' she said. 'Makes it nice and comfortable in there. My Alan always said I needed a bit of extra weight, that I'd feel every kick. He was right you know, the cheeky old sod. There's me eating celery like a starving horse, when I should have been on the scones. You got a man in your life?'

Edith was still trying to figure out a) whether Barbara was insulting her weight or berating her own; and b) whether or not her first assessment was actually correct, and the geriatric shop owner really was some kind of fairy-tale witch.

'Ah, no. Not right now.'

Barbara cackled. 'Such a pretty thing like you. Won't be long, mark my words. You know what they say about November in Trenton, don't you?'

'Um, no?'

'Love comes in the leaves that fall from the trees.' She poked a finger at Edith's lap, where a number of fallen leaves had settled during the last gust of wind, and which Edith was yet to brush away. 'And by the look of the colour of those, you're in for untold riches.'

'Right.'

Barbara grinned. 'Go on, have another scone. This old basket's heavy, and there aren't many folk around on a weekday. I just had to get my baking skills up to scratch for the festival next weekend.'

'You mean the harvest festival? Are you going?'

'Not missed a single one in all my life,' Barbara said. 'You know it's the seventy-fifth anniversary this year? My old bread stand has been there for the last sixty, and I helped Pa and Ma before that. All homemade, all by hand.' She gave a wispy little sigh. 'I don't have the strength in my fingers much these days, though. You ever tried kneading dough for bread with needles under your nails? That's what it feels like with arthritis.'

'That's too bad. I mean, I could help you, if you like. My parents have a—' *Food mixer. But they don't now, because James is renting their house, and that includes everything in it.* '—friend with big hands,' she said instead. Then, thinking of Max, she added, 'And she has a friend with big hands. And there's a kitchen up at Trenton Manor with lots of space, so we could help you.'

As long as James doesn't find out….

'Why, that would be most helpful. Trenton Manor, you say? You're that postcard girl, aren't you? The one with the giant friend.' Barbara grinned. 'I bet she could knead dough for England.'

'I'm sure she'd be happy to help.'

'Trenton Manor.' Barbara stared down at the river,

nodding slowly. Jam was starting to run through Edith's fingers, and she wondered whether the old woman would mind if she started to eat.

'That's right,' she said, as a glob of jam dropped onto her jeans. 'That big house, just up the hill.'

'Trenton Manor.' Barbara continued to nod. 'I remember that place, back in the day. Beautiful, but tainted. Through and through.'

'Tainted? What do you mean?'

'Lived in by the heirs of a cheat,' Barbara said. 'A pauper became a lord, and a lord became a pauper. And over the years, everyone forgot.' She leaned forwards until she was so close to Edith that she was nearly blocking out the sun. 'Everyone that is, except my old Pa.'

'Um … forgot what?'

'The answer's right there, paraded in front of the world,' Barbara continued cryptically. 'Pickles … not his name, was it? The man was a canner over in Willow River, my Pa said. Made the finest chutney this side of Exeter, but that wasn't enough, was it? Always wanted more, didn't he?' She leaned even closer, lowering her voice to a harsh whisper. 'Not a name for a lord, is it, Pickles?'

'I wouldn't know,' Edith said.

'Ah, but my Pa did. And he swore until his deathbed that Trenton Manor's secrets were held within its walls. Cleaning the place up, are you?'

'Something like that.'

'You haven't spotted any hidden staircases, any revolving bookcases?'

'No, none,' Edith said. 'Just the usual dusty corridors and rooms filled with cobwebs.'

'Have you seen the ghost?'

Edith grimaced. 'Not yet.'

'The ghost of an aggrieved man. One cheated out of

his fortune.'

The cream was following the jam down onto Edith's jeans. She was just about to throw manners under the bus and stuff one of the scones into her mouth when Barbara suddenly pulled away. 'Secrets,' the old woman said. 'There's no house that old that doesn't have its secrets. And if you're up there sorting through the place, no better time to find out.'

Barbara turned and stumbled off, muttering to herself. Edith watched her cross the road and head up the path along the river, then she got to work eating the scones before the fillings were no longer fillings and her jeans resembled the kitchens at Wimbledon on finals day. They certainly didn't taste past their best. In fact, they were pretty much the best scones Edith had ever tasted; soft and fluffy, just sweet enough. And with the jam and cream also having a homemade taste, Edith found a little cheerful glow starting to build up inside.

(Unless it's the poison, of course.)

Life didn't seem so bad. Sure, she was homeless, without any money, a boyfriend, or a full-time job; her family had abandoned her, and her only friend was loved up, but otherwise, things were great. The sun was bright, the river was making a pretty gurgle, and the leaves showering down off the towering maple trees glittered and shone. Even the chilly wind wasn't too bad.

As she walked back up the hill to Trenton Manor, she had a spring in her step. While it was possibly a sugar rush, she liked to think she had a renewed sense of purpose and outlook. Things could definitely be worse.

She wondered whether Stephanie was back yet. As she went in through the front door, though, she didn't have to wonder long; the great, gasping sobs coming from the kitchen up the corridor couldn't belong to anyone else.

18

SECRETS

Stephanie was inconsolable, head on her hands, sobbing dramatically as she sat at the kitchen table. Edith ran over, sat down alongside and tried to put a hand around Stephanie's massive shoulders, even though she could only reach halfway.

'It's all right,' she said, patting Stephanie on the back. 'Sometimes these things don't work out. You'd only been seeing each other a couple of days, so it's not like you were in too deep. If you'd been together longer, it would be much worse.'

Stephanie looked up. Her face, bright red, shone with tears.

'He wants me to meet his mother,' she said.

'What? He didn't dump you?'

Stephanie shook her head. 'No,' she wailed. 'He wants me to meet his mother. And his dad. And his brothers and sisters. What am I going to do?'

'Um … meet them?'

'I can't! I'm a monster!'

'You're not a monster. You're just tall. You're what, six foot two?'

'Three. Six-three.'

'But he's tall too, isn't he?'

'Six-five.'

'So, perhaps his mother's like … a basketball player or something. Perhaps they're all tall.'

'But she'll hate me!'

'Why?'

'Because I'll go around there and I'll get nervous and I'll want to steal something, and I'll have to do the chicken thing so that I don't, and they'll think I should be in a mental hospital—'

Edith patted Stephanie on the shoulder. 'Calm down. I think you're overreacting. Max wouldn't ask you to meet his family if he didn't really like you.'

'But … I can't.'

'Why not?'

'I'm scared.'

Edith smiled. 'I'll make some coffee. Or should we steal something out of the wine cellar?'

'No! No more stealing. Coffee's fine.' Stephanie wiped a hand across her eyes. 'I'm sorry. It just came as a shock. I'm not used to this.'

'You'll be fine. By the way, I have a favour to ask. I kind of volunteered us to help Barbara from the shop down in Trenton make some homemade bread for the harvest festival next weekend. Do you know how to knead dough?'

'I helped the woman at the hostel do it once,' Stephanie said. 'She told me to just imagine it was someone I didn't like.'

'That would work. Perhaps you could ask Max to help too? We can borrow this kitchen. I doubt Lord Pickles would mind.'

'Sure. When?'

'Well, I'll have to check with Barbara, but the festival is on Saturday, so maybe Thursday or Friday?'

'I'll tell Max. We can probably get Anthony to help too.'

'Ah, I'm sure he's busy. Three will be enough.'

Stephanie gave her a withering look. 'Is there something you're not telling me?'

Edith thought about her encounter with James and Anthony, then Barbara's strange words.

'No,' she said. 'Everything's fine.'

∽

After coffee, they got back down to their work. Having felt like they had both slacked off a little, Edith threw herself into it for the next couple of days, and Stephanie, perhaps preoccupied by the upcoming meeting with Max's family, was lost in her thoughts. Edith concentrated on cleaning the upper floors, while Stephanie hauled things labelled for disposal down into the entrance hall, and worked in the garden, cutting back the overgrown hedges, strimming the grass of lawns that had become wild meadows.

Tuesday morning was bin day. While everything large would need to be taken away by a proper skip service, they had more than thirty bags of bits and bobs to put out. One by one, they hauled them up the long drive to the collection point just outside the main gates. As Edith set the last bag down, Stephanie who had done two at a time, offered to go back and make coffee. Edith, exhausted, paused for a moment to recover her breath. As she stared at the mountain of rubbish bags, a low growl announced the approach of a car. A moment later, James's Porsche glided into view, pulling up alongside her.

A tinted window slid down, and James, wearing sunglasses and a suit that were both probably expensive, leaned out.

'Oh, hey there. How's everything going?' He glanced back at the pile of bin bags and grinned. 'Not throwing away any family secrets, are you?'

'No. About two hundred telephone bills from the nineteen fifties is about as exciting as it gets,' Edith said.

'That's good to know. You're doing a fine job, by the way. I was up at the hospital yesterday and gave Grandfather Arnold a rundown of your progress. I'm afraid he's a bit out of it at the moment, but he kind of smiled.' James shrugged. 'Well, more of a twitch, but it was good enough. We won't be opening the will for a couple more weeks, though. He's hanging in there.'

'You must be heartbroken. All those cars you could buy.'

'I know, it's very selfish of him, isn't it?' He smirked. 'So, are we still on for Saturday?'

'Um, no.'

'Really? You know the other day was just a bit of silliness, wasn't it? Kind of like a pre-lovers' tiff?'

'We're not anything lovers, and we never will be.'

James sighed. 'Look, we got off on the wrong foot. How about we just make it a friendship date? Two mates hanging out, no strings attached, no pressure, and just take it from there?'

'No, I'll be all right.'

James's smile dropped. 'Look, I'm sorry. I should be more understanding. It's the class difference, isn't it? You know it's just money, don't you? And I mean, the title is just hereditary. It doesn't really have any meaning. It's just something you select from a drop-down menu when you sign up for something online. You know, most people choose Mr. or Mrs., or Doctor, or Reverend … I have to choose Lord. Well, at least after Grandfather gives up the ghost. You don't have to be intimidated. I'm sure there are loads of aristocrats who've hooked up with people below them you know, servants and the like. Most of them probably just as side gigs, but a few have probably ended up married. It's not a big deal.'

Edith wondered whether she could grab the closest bag of rubbish and empty it into his car before he managed to get the window up. She looked around, wondering which one was food waste.

'Look, I don't mean to be rude, but I'm kind of busy right now.'

James lifted an eyebrow. 'Are you sure? It looked to me like you were taking a break. I'm not sure what Grandfather put in his contract, but industry standard is two fifteen-minute breaks a day.' He grinned, leaving Edith unsure whether he was actually joking or being as tight as it really appeared. 'Look, let's get our date back on this Saturday, and we can discuss it.' He lifted an eyebrow. 'What do you say to three breaks a day, at no financial loss?'

'Actually, there's a harvest festival down in Trenton,' Edith said. 'I've offered to help out.' It was more or less true, after all.

'Really? They still do that little thing? I remember Dad taking me down there once when I was a kid, you know, before the lion and all that. Can't have been more than twenty people there. And I got food poisoning after eating a dodgy scone. I was on the toilet all night.'

'How lovely.'

'Really, I'm sure you'd enjoy a night out with me far more. And if you still want to see that harvest festival, I'm sure if I made a large enough donation they'd be happy to move it to a different day.' He clicked his fingers. 'Money talks.'

'I thought you said it was just money.'

'Well, for some people it is. For others, its power. Don't you find that attractive? So many people do.'

Edith grimaced, and looked down at her empty wrist. 'Well, I'm afraid that's my fifteen minutes up. I'd better get back to clearing out your grandfather's junk.'

'I suppose I'll see you on Fridayfor payday, if not before,' James said.

'I'll be counting down the seconds.'

James clicked his fingers again, then revved the engine. 'I have no doubt about it,' he said, then sped off up the road, the Porsche so large it took up almost the road's entire width. Edith prayed for a tractor to appear around the corner up ahead, but sadly, today didn't appear to be her lucky day.

When she got back to the house, Stephanie was standing in the entrance, waiting for her, a mobile phone held in her hand. Her face was pale, her bottom lip trembling.

'Max just called,' she said. 'He asked me to meet him for lunch. I think he's going to break up with me.'

Edith laughed. 'I doubt that very much.'

'He wanted to go down to the pub in Trenton. He said Tuesday is curry and a pint day.'

'Ha, yeah, really sounds like he wants to break up with you.'

Stephanie's expression didn't change. 'I told him I was bringing a mate. That's you, by the way. I thought he wouldn't dare break up with me in front of someone else.'

'Possibly not, but I really don't think—'

'And he said if I was bringing a mate, then he was going to bring a mate, too.'

'Right, so—'

'I think he's trying to downgrade it from dates to mates,' Stephanie said.

'Look, I think you're overreacting.'

'Do you think so?'

'Just a bit. Plus, if he's downgrading from "dates to mates", then you called it first, didn't you? By the way, who's his mate? Is it—'

'Probably Rick.'

'Oh, well, in that case, I suppose—'

'What?'

Edith just smiled. 'Have you ever stolen a wheel off a Porsche?'

'No.'

'Do you want to try? Look, I just had a pretty rubbish encounter with James, out by the er, rubbish. I think we should finish up what we're doing and then head down to the pub, get a head start on Max and uh, Rick.'

'Sure.'

Worried that James would start spying on them, Edith put in a burst of extra effort before their planned lunch break, trying to make up for whatever time they spent skiving off in the pub. So, so much junk. Every drawer or cupboard was filled with dog-eared magazines, books with faded covers, musty, moth-eaten clothes. Some of it had been labelled for keeping of course, and she thought the National Trust and English Heritage would like a sort through, but much of it was fit only for the bin. Dozens of folded sheets, so old they fell apart when Edith tried to take them out of a cupboard. An entire room full of stacked, woodworm-infested chairs. Boxes of old photographs left too close to a leaking pipe, reduced to a hardened lump of paper mâché.

There were of course, a few gems that Pickles had

missed. One cupboard revealed a pair of packaged oil paintings that looked at least a couple of hundred years old. Stephanie did an internet search for the signature and swore they were two paintings stolen from a London gallery more than a hundred years earlier.

They were still debating whether to call the police, call their mothers, or do nothing, when Edith pushed aside a rail of tatty business suits and found a key hanging on a chain at the back of a wardrobe.

'I wonder what this opens?' she said, holding up the large, ornate key.

Both girls looked up at the ceiling.

'Let's go and check,' Stephanie said.

Up on the roof, they approached the locked door with trepidation. It was the only room in the house they were yet to find a way into. What possible surprise might it spring? They'd found all sorts, from a room full of live, hanging bats to the skeleton of a horse in a glass display case hidden underneath a sheet, something almost as horrifying as the monstrous displays in Edith's parents' cellar.

'Pound says it's the mummified body of one of Pickles's ancestors,' Stephanie said.

'All right. Well, I reckon it'll have a chest of stolen jewels.'

'Booby traps?'

'Maybe. We'd better duck when we open it in case there are spring triggers for arrows hidden in the walls.'

'This is so like Indiana Jones,' Stephanie said.

Edith stuck the key into the lock. 'Right, put your hand over mine, and we'll turn it together. Don't forget to duck.'

'Okay.'

'On three. One … two … three—'

They turned the key, the lock mechanism moving with

a dusty clump. The door, gummed up with leaf litter along the bottom, resisted their push at first, then gave in a sudden rush which had both girls stumbling into the room.

'So much for ducking,' Edith said. 'If there were arrows in the walls, we'd both be dead.'

'Looks like we got lucky,' Stephanie replied. 'No snakes on the floor or bugs on the walls.'

'In fact, there isn't really anything, is there?'

The room, at first glance, was something of a disappointment. Windowless, it was no bigger than the kitchen at Edith's parents' place, a few steps across. Made entirely of stone, apart from a single table pushed against one wall, it was empty. No shelves, no cupboards, not even a chair. No nooks nor cubbyholes, nowhere to hide any treasure, mummified remains, or anything else of interest.

It looked like a big store cupboard, perhaps where the outdoor furniture for the rooftop patio could have been kept.

Edith couldn't help but sigh with disappointment, but Stephanie pointed at the table.

'What's that?' she said. 'There's something on it. It looks like glass.'

They went over to the table together. It was ancient, made of hardwood, perhaps oak or mahogany, ornately carved, varnished, durable. What lay on top was of most interest, however. A large pane of glass, slightly off-centre, meaning it was not part of the table's design, but had been placed there by someone. The years had covered it with dust, so Edith pulled her sleeve over her hand and wiped a line through the grey fluff, wondering what was beneath.

'There's writing,' Stephanie said. 'Looks like something underneath. Here, use this.' She pulled a handkerchief out of her pocket and handed it to Edith.

Being very careful not to move the glass, Edith used the

handkerchief to clear away the dust. Beneath the glass was a rectangle of paper adorned with ornate copperplate handwriting in black ink, now so faded as to be barely legible. Edith stared at it, unable to pick out anything other than a number at the top: 1885. In fact, as she started to pick letters out of the script, she realised it wasn't even English at all.

'I think it's Latin,' she said, 'judging from the look of some of those words. What on earth do you think it is?'

Stephanie pointed at a word near the bottom. 'I think that says "Pickles", but I'm not sure. We'd better not move it. Do you think we should tell James or Arnold? It could be some historical family record.'

Edith pulled out her phone and took a picture of the document. 'Who knows? I think we should leave it right here for now, just in case. I mean, who knows how long it's been since anyone was in here?'

'We can discuss it over curry,' Stephanie said. 'That's if Max doesn't dump me.'

Edith checked the time on her phone's display. 'Well, I think it's about time we went and found out.'

19
PUB JOKES

THE MORNING'S CHILL STILL LINGERED IN THE SHADOWS, but the sun was warm, beaming out of a clear autumn sky as they made their way down the hill into Trenton. A few last golden leaves clung to the maple trees, and when a gust of wind sent a shower fluttering around them, Edith told Stephanie to catch one. As Stephanie opened her hands to reveal a shining golden leaf, Edith said, 'You know what they say, don't you? Love comes in the leaves that fall from the trees.'

'Did you make that up?'

Edith laughed. 'No, I heard it from Barbara. The woman who owns the shop? Maybe that leaf will be good luck for you with Max.'

Stephanie pressed it to her face. 'I hope so.'

They were early, so got a table inside the bar and ordered a couple of coffees. While Edith was trying to calm an excitable Stephanie, who was still convinced she was about to get dumped, Matt came over with a flyer in his hands.

'Hey, girls. This is for the festival at the weekend. I

hope you'll be there. By the way, I don't suppose I could ask a favour?'

'Sure,' Edith said, taking the flyer, which was headed with the words Trenton Harvest Festival 2024, and had a number of pictures overlaying each other: one of a line of maple trees, another of food stalls, a man ringing a bell, a group of dancers on a stage.

'We're a bit short of acts this year,' Matt said. 'Comes with living in a part of the country where everyone's drawing their pension. I don't suppose either of you can sing or play anything?'

Edith glanced at Stephanie, who was frantically shaking her head. Sweat was beading on Stephanie's brow, and the table had begun to rock where her foot was tapping against the leg.

'Yeah, we can,' Edith said. 'Stephanie can—'

'Edith used to be a comedian!' Stephanie blurted, loud enough to mask anything Edith might have said.

Matt's eyes lit up. 'Really? We've never had a comedian before.'

'Ah, not really. I just did it a few times at university. Just for fun, you know.'

'That's all this is, really. Just for fun. Thanks, that would be great.'

'Ah—'

'Can I put you down?'

No, no, no, Edith's mind was screaming, but she heard herself muttering, 'Sure, if you like.'

My chance to come out of Ellen's shadow? Ha. More likely the moment I put my silly dreams to rest. Might as well get it over with!

Wishing for moral support, Edith looked at Stephanie, willing her friend to join her, but Stephanie just shook her head.

'I'm not good at anything,' she said.

'That's too bad, but never mind,' Matt said. 'If you know of anyone, give them a shout. At the moment the headline act is me and Daniel up at the farm doing a magic show. Last year we tried to make a chicken disappear, but the bottom fell out of the tank and it made a break for freedom. It didn't go down well.' He shrugged. 'Lucy—that's the chicken—is this year's festival mascot.'

'Sounds … fun.'

Matt smiled. 'Well, we should level up this year with a bit of comedy. Dan and me won't have to headline.'

'What? You want me to … headline?'

'Yeah, that would be great. We'll have you last on. You can have half an hour. Will that be long enough?'

'She'd be delighted,' Stephanie said.

Edith's vision blurred. 'Uh,' she muttered.

'Awesome. I'll get the new flyers printed up. Edith….?'

'Davies,' Stephanie finished, as Edith just gave a froglike croak.

'Oh, yeah, are you one of those from up by the main road? Rufus's girl?' Matt's eyes lit up. 'Wow, you wrote *Transcendent*, didn't you? Oh my goodness. I loved that show. We'll make you the guest of honour this year. With someone so famous, the turnout will be great. I think we only got twenty people last year.'

'You're talking about the other one,' Edith said, just as Stephanie, raising her voice to drown Edith out, said, 'She'll be delighted to come. She might even give you a talk about life in Hollywood.'

'Life about having a famous sister who works in Hollywood!' Edith called as

Matt went back to the bar to get their drinks, leaving her unsure whether he had even heard. With a scowl, she leaned forwards over the table. 'What are you doing?' she hissed at Stephanie. 'He thinks I'm Ellen! I don't know anything about TV!'

'Now's your chance to share a bit of your sister's limelight,' Stephanie said. 'Go on, it'll be fun.'

'And meanwhile you with the awesome piano skills pretends you couldn't even spell Yamaha if it was tattooed on your forehead.'

Stephanie gave an awkward shrug, then suddenly her eyes widened in surprise. 'Oh my God, here's Max. What do I do?'

'Tell the truth?'

'I need to … to … cluck, cluck, cluck!'

Stephanie broke out into a chicken gesture just as Matt returned with their coffees. He stared at her, then smiled. 'Are you going to do a double act?'

'Thinking about it,' Edith said, glaring at Stephanie. Behind them, the bar door opened, and Max came in, followed by Rick, with Marge trotting along on a lead behind him. Edith felt a strange sense of relief as she watched the door swing closed, only to open again as Anthony followed them in. Something inside her gave a little jump. Something else was tugging at her, and it took a moment to realise it was Stephanie, who had hold of her arm and was pulling her out of the seat.

'Conference,' Stephanie said, dragging Edith off in the direction of the Ladies. Max and Anthony looked bemused, while Rick turned to Matt, let out a chuckle, and said, 'Pub with the most watered-down beer in Devon, eh? Going for the again, ten years in a row?'

Matt grinned. 'It's the bag,' he said. 'Quicker than you can say, "a pint of tap, please."'

'What have you got that's not watered down?'

'New shipment of Local in from St Austell,' he said. 'No one's stayed awake longer than three pints yet.'

'Game on. Pint each for the boys, and I'll have a half.'

Stephanie slammed the toilet door shut, cutting off Matt's response. She rounded on Edith with a look of horror in her eyes.

'I don't think I can do this,' she said.

'Oh, I'm sure you can. What can't be done is me standing on a stage this Saturday and telling half an hour's worth of jokes while pretending to be my sister.'

Stephanie put a hand into her pocket and pulled out a salt cellar.

'It's starting,' she said.

At the look of utter horror in Stephanie's eyes, Edith's intensity faltered. She smiled, patted Stephanie on the arm and said, 'I have an idea. After lunch, why don't you suggest a walk along the river? You know, just you and Max? It'll be far more romantic, the leaves will calm you down, and there won't be anything to steal because everything's kind of attached to the ground.'

'We have to get through lunch first. I wish I could just run away.'

'What, like your dad did?'

A tear beaded in Stephanie's eye, and Edith's heart lurched. She felt like the worst person in the world.

'Look, I'm really sorry. I put my foot in it again. I didn't mean it—'

Stephanie stood up straight, the top of her head not far off the ceiling. For a moment Edith thought Stephanie meant to exercise some painful wrestling finishing move on her, but instead Stephanie puffed out her chest, took a deep breath and forced a resilient smile.

'You're right,' she said. 'I have to face my troubles. I just wish Dad….'

Before Edith could say anything, Stephanie burst into a flood of tears. Edith attempted to hug her, but it was like trying to hug a hedgerow, and she ended up just patting Stephanie on the back. Just as she was thinking that perhaps they could try climbing out of the toilet window, however, the door banged open and Barbara stepped through the doorway, wearing her pointed hat. Leaning on a cane, she glared at first Edith and then Stephanie, eyes narrowed.

'Well, what do we have here then?' she said. 'Pull yourselves together. I can't handle all three of them on my own, can I? Fifty years ago, a doddle, but not anymore. Why do you think I walk with a stick?'

∽

It turned out that Rick, afraid of being the odd man out, had invited Barbara to their lunch party. As the old woman flirted shamelessly with the slightly younger, but still geriatric timber merchant owner, Stephanie began to relax in Max's company. Edith was pleased to see her friend put the salt cellar back, and hold on to Max's hands instead.

However, the obvious coupling off of Max and Stephanie, and the old-times chit-chat of Rick and Barbara, left Edith in an uncomfortable situation with Anthony.

'So ... how has life been since I pushed you into the school pond?' she said, a glass of wine having loosened her tongue a little.

Anthony grinned. 'Pretty much an upwards climb. You can't get much lower than all that gunky pondweed, can you? I mean, I don't think they'd ever cleaned it. I was picking bits of weed out of my shoes for weeks. How about you?'

Edith shrugged. 'That was probably the pinnacle of my school bullying career. I became good after that.'

'I remember.'

'Do you?'

Anthony smiled. It was a nice smile, she had to admit. 'Yes. I mean, you were kind of in the cool girl's group, so I wasn't ever going to talk to you, but I watched you from time to time. I always wondered what became of you. Sometimes I'd bump into your dad out doing some jogging or yoga or whatever and ask him how you were doing. He said you were living it up in the city.'

Edith grimaced, and tucked a loose strand of hair behind her ear. 'Yeah, he meant Brentwell. It's marginally bigger than Willow River, but you know, it's a low bar.'

'Did you ever become a nurse?'

'A nurse? Ha, no chance.'

'You know, back in Sixth Form, some of us boys used to predict what you girls would end up as. Pretty much everyone thought you were going to be a nurse.'

Edith's cheeks flushed. 'Really? Why was that?'

Anthony shrugged. 'You were always kind. I mean, apart from the pond thing, but you know, you were like, twelve?'

Edith sighed. 'Eleven.'

Antony grinned. 'And you were always fussing about.'

'What? I never fussed about!'

'You wouldn't sit down for five minutes.'

'I'm not sure whether to feel complimented or insulted.'

'Ah, you'd have made a great nurse.'

'You think?'

'I definitely don't think you're destined to spend your whole life as a cleaner.'

'Well, I was a secretary and receptionist for a therapist. I thought I was pretty good at it. Turns out she wasn't all that good at her job, had to close down, and here I am, cleaning houses for rich old people.'

'Ah, life gives us the ups and downs, eh. You'll be fine.'

'What about you? Are you planning to carry planks of wood forever?'

Anthony smiled, and his eyes seemed to twinkle. Edith feared her words might be taken as a veiled insult, but Anthony said, 'Never underestimate the value of a bit of physical labour. Sitting at a desk all day just gives you a Vitamin D deficiency.'

'My arms have never ached so much since I started at Trenton Manor,' Edith said. 'It's a shame I get paid half as much as I did for filing bits of paper and typing numbers into a screen.'

'You're getting paid in experience,' Anthony said. 'I bet that place has some secrets.'

Edith remembered the strange rooftop room with the letter underneath the sheet of glass, and was just about to show Anthony the picture on her phone, when Rick clapped her on the shoulder.

'Maid, I hear from Matt over there that you're doing us a stand-up routine at the festival next weekend. Go on, tell us a joke.'

Edith swallowed, trying to channel the inner comedian that had drawn the occasional laugh out of groups of drunks in the university bar. 'Actually,' she said, 'I was thinking of standing down.'

Rick leaned back in his chair, chortling with laughter. 'Maid, you're going to destroy this place.'

Stephanie and Max were both smiling. Even Anthony looked amused. Barbara, however, frowned and said, 'I don't get it.'

'It wasn't a joke.'

'I don't get that one either.'

'Maid, go on, tell us another,' Rick said. 'A longer one this time.'

Everyone was looking at her expectantly. 'Ah....' She closed her eyes for a moment, wondering how her sister did it with such ease. Ellen, who had been perfect at everything she did, who had been writing screenplays at thirteen, who had more awards than Edith currently had pounds in her bank account. The few jokes Edith had written that she could remember sounded as stale as a packet of digestive biscuits not sealed up properly.

'I was at the park,' she said, opening her eyes, letting herself ramble on, wondering what would come out. 'And I saw this dog. When the owner smiled at me, I asked him … ah … if his dog was genetically engineered … and … and he said, uh, why? And I said … ah well, it's a, ah … Labrador, isn't it?'

Rick burst into laughter, pushed himself away from the table and would have crashed to the floor had Max not caught his chair and hauled him back upright.

'Ah, maid, you're killing me.'

Edith, sweat beading on her brow, just smiled.

'You're a natural,' Anthony said.

'I just made it up on the spot. I didn't think it was that funny.'

'If you can do that, just think what you could do if you put your mind to it.'

Edith shrugged. 'Maybe.'

Max and Stephanie excused themselves to take a walk outside. Rick, still chuckling, hobbled over to the bar. After a quick scowl at both of them, Barbara snapped something about the powder room.

Suddenly Edith and Anthony were alone.

'So … you're going to perform at the harvest festival?' Anthony said.

Edith flapped her hands. 'I was hoping to get Stephanie to volunteer,' she said. 'But it backfired. Did you know she can play piano like an angel? I couldn't believe it. But she just backed me into a corner, let me set myself up to make a fool of myself.'

'Max told me she has some confidence issues. He said she keeps running off and giving him the silent treatment. He really likes her, though. I've never seen him swoon over anyone before.'

'She was swooning over him, too.'

'Looks like they're perfect for each other.'

'Yes.'

Edith had been looking at the table, but as Anthony reached for his pint glass and took a drink, she looked up, studying him. Rough around the edges, but handsome in a woodsman sort of way. Muscular, strong, yet with a sensitive centre—

She jerked as he turned, catching her studying him. Edith stared at her hands, her heart thundering. Had she been checking him out. He wasn't her type at all—

'I was thinking … if you wanted to practise some of those jokes of yours before your big performance on Saturday, I'd be willing to listen. Perhaps we could get something to eat, maybe Thursday night…?'

Edith found herself leaning forwards in a kind of positive gesture, but her tongue had swollen to the size of a small moon and no words would come out. She looked at him, trying to give her answer with her eyes, just as Rick returned from the bar and clapped Anthony on the shoulder.

'Right, lad. Back to work for us.'

Edith tried to make some kind of sound that would give Anthony his answer, but all she could do was stare at him as he got out of the seat, smiled at her, and followed

Rick to the door. Turning back, he gave her a little wave, then they were outside, walking away towards Rick's van.

'Yes,' Edith croaked too late.

'Oh, just me and you now, is it?' Barbara said, appearing at Edith's shoulder so suddenly she could have stepped out of a puff of smoke. 'Never mind. I suppose we'll just have to have a girl's chat, won't we?'

20

CHASING SECRETS

'...AND THEN I SAID, "WELL, YOU'RE A COB-LER, aren't you?"'

Stephanie just stared. 'Why don't you click your fingers or something when you want me to laugh?'

'You don't get it at all?'

'It's not that I don't get it, it's just a bit weird.'

Edith sighed. 'Look, I only agreed to do it because I was trying to encourage you to do something. Unlike you or my sister, I'm completely talentless.'

'You're not talentless. That one about the puppy in the basket was a bit funny.'

'A bit funny. Yeah, that's the problem. I'm definitely either brave or stupid, there's no question of that. But funny, nope. And talented … nope. You, though. You're amazing. You should just give it a go. As Matt said, there'll probably only be about twenty people there.'

Stephanie grinned. 'If we can get at least ten of them to laugh when you click your fingers, that should be enough.'

Edith sighed. 'This is ridiculous. I'll never be my sister.

I'll go down and see Matt in the morning, tell him I'm cancelling.'

'No, don't do that.'

'I have to. I'm going to humiliate myself.'

'Just try.'

'Says the girl who won't.'

Stephanie looked down. 'You don't understand. I just … can't. The only person I ever played for was my dad.'

'I thought you said you played at the hostel you were staying in?'

'Yes, but that was just practising. It wasn't … *playing*.'

'I don't….' Edith began, but then remembered the postcard she had seen in Stephanie's room. 'I'm so sorry about what I said about your dad,' she said. 'When he left, it hurt, didn't it?'

'It … changed everything,' Stephanie said.

'I … I … saw a postcard in your room,' Edith said. 'I'm sorry, I wasn't being nosy, I was just collecting those other ones to take back. It was … it was from your dad, wasn't it?'

Stephanie's eyes filled with tears. 'I received it six months after he left,' she said. 'It was sent to my old house, but the new owners brought it round. My mum wasn't there, otherwise she might have taken it and got rid of it, I don't know. They handed it directly to me. It was him telling me where to find him, and I've always dreamed of going out there, but I've never had the money. I think that's one reason I steal … in my mind I have this idea that I could sell everything, make the money to fly out to South America and find my dad.' She shrugged. 'At least that was part of it.' She shook her head. 'I don't know. All I know is, that whatever happened to him, it wasn't because of me. He loved me. I know he did. At night, when I lie awake, I can still see the way he looked at me, and it was there, in his eyes.'

It was Edith's turn to wipe away a tear. 'I'm so sorry.'

Stephanie shrugged. 'It is what it is. I just wish … things could be different.'

'Maybe they can. Look, I don't know how much it costs to go out to South America, but I'll help you if you like.' Edith smiled. 'After all, it was me who my dad was signing up for this. Think of it as a Christmas bonus for helping me.'

'We're barely being paid enough to survive as it is,' Stephanie said. 'It's really kind of you to offer, but I can't accept anything from you. Don't even try to change my mind.'

Edith sighed. 'Perhaps if we really did steal the tyres off James's Porsche and sold them? They must be worth a fortune.'

Stephanie grinned. 'Crime doesn't pay. Trust me. If there's one thing I've figured out, it's that.'

'Right, I suppose we'd better get back to work, otherwise we'll incur the wrath of the Pickles family's heir.'

'You know, I was thinking about that thing we found up in that secret room,' Stephanie said. 'I can't help but wonder what it says.'

'It's probably an 18th century bank statement. But yeah, I was wondering that, too. It's a real mystery, isn't it? You know, it's the kind of thing my sister would love. She writes television series about this kind of stuff.'

'I tried to translate it using my phone, but the writing's not clear enough. You don't know anyone who can read Latin, do you?'

Edith shook her head. 'No, but … I know someone I could ask.'

Leaving Stephanie to gather her cleaning materials,

Edith went out to the front entrance where the phone connection was best, and called up her old work colleague, Roger Westerly.

'Edith, dear, is that you?'

'Hi, Roger! How are you doing?'

'Enjoying retirement for the most part,' he told her. 'Although I miss seeing your cheery face in the morning, and listening to your questionable jokes. The old dear on BBC News doesn't have the same charm. What are you doing these days? Did you manage to find something?'

'Well, long story short, yes and no. I'm currently working on a short-term contract clearing out and cleaning Trenton Manor ready for it to go on the market.'

'Are you really? How bizarre. Isn't it haunted?'

'We've had worse to worry about than a few ghosts, but we're slowly getting there. I just wanted to ask you something. I know you were big on your classic books and all that, and I just wondered if you knew anyone who could read Latin.'

'Huh. Back in the day I did a little myself, but those days are long gone. You need to speak to Lawrence over at the Brentwell Library. If there's anyone around who'll know, he will. Actually, he's an old mate so I'll give him a call. What's it about?'

'We found an old document written in Latin in a tiny sealed-up room that's only accessible via the roof. The only thing we could figure out was the year, 1885, and the text was too squiggly and faded for any translation apps on our phones. It all looked very secretive, though.'

'Have you told the owner?'

Edith grimaced. 'No ... not yet. The man who hired us is currently in hospital. His grandson is hovering around, having rented out my parents' place. He's kind of ... unsavoury.'

'A bit of an arse?'

Edith chuckled. 'Yeah, that would be about it. Showing up all the time in his Porsche, then scrimping on our pay for arbitrary reasons. If there was anything else we could do, we would probably quit. A job's a job, though, isn't it?'

'You said "we". Are you working with someone else?'

'Yeah, her name's Stephanie Mansfield. She was lodging with my parents.'

'Oh, for a moment, I thought your sister might have come back for a visit. I started watching her most recent show last week. *Transcendent*, isn't it?'

Edith sighed. 'Yeah, that's the one.'

Roger gave a gentle chuckle. 'I couldn't really get into it. Not my thing.'

'You're just being kind.'

'I know it's hard for you coping with a famous sister, but as I told you a thousand times, stop worrying about her, and start worrying about yourself. You're so capable, Edith. You could do anything you want.'

Edith smiled. Roger had always had a knack for saying exactly the right thing. 'Talking of which … I somehow volunteered to do a stand-up comedy routine at Trenton Harvest Festival next weekend. You don't happen to know any good jokes, do you? Mine are a bit … stale.'

'Oh dear, what have you got yourself into? I'll definitely have to stop by and watch that. No problem, I've got a couple. Have you got a pen and paper nearby?'

～

'There you go,' Barbara said, dumping a linen sack down on the ground in front of Edith and Stephanie, next to a stack of plastic containers and a couple of cartons of milk. Behind her, an ancient van spluttered as it idled on the gravel. 'That's the last of them. You know how to make bread? Yeast in warm water. Three parts flour to one part water, a dash of milk, and a nob of butter. A sprinkle of salt per handful of dough, and half a teaspoon of sugar. Knead it like your ex-husband just gambled away your jewellery and you don't want him to forget. Got that? Let it rise for an hour, then put it in those plastic buckets over there, and make sure it's covered. That way it'll keep until I can get it baked.'

Edith glanced at Stephanie who lifted an eyebrow. 'How much will this make?' she said.

'Three hundred bread rolls, give or take,' Barbara said. 'We don't want to be short. And you never know if this festival could be your last. You have to go out with a bang, don't you?'

'I suppose so.' Edith shrugged as Stephanie grinned.

'I'll be up with the rest in the morning.'

'The … rest?'

Barbara grinned. 'Didn't think this was all, did you? Got a whole parish to cook for, if they all come out. This is just the rolls. We have the loaves to do, too. Plus, I always like to have a few scones, so you can mix that dough up for me as well, while you're at it. Don't worry, you girls have got the easy bit. You've just got to pour the water.' She gave a gappy grin. 'I have to turn it into wine.'

Barbara climbed back into her little truck and chuntered off, leaving Edith and Stephanie staring at the industrial-sized pile of ingredients. It was only Wednesday, a day earlier than expected, but Barbara had clearly decided to go large with her stall this year. Edith stared at the heap, wondering how they would get it all turned into bread dough both while continuing with their work and without James finding out that they were turning Trenton Manor into an impromptu bakery.

Stephanie, however, looked delighted. 'Let's give Max and Anthony a call,' she said. 'We could invite them round for dinner. I don't think Barbara would notice if we skimmed a little of this dough and made some pizzas, would she?' Before Edith could respond, Stephanie tucked her hands under her arms and began to chant, 'Cluck, cluck! Cluck, cluck, cluck!'

Edith stared at her. 'On one condition,' she said.

'What?'

'You play the piano. Not just for Max or me, but for all of us.'

21

PIANO RECITAL

'So, I was in the supermarket the other day, and I picked up one of those bottles of tomato sauce,' Edith said, slapping a fist into her palm for emphasis. Sat around the table while Edith paced back and forth as though prowling a stage, Stephanie, Max and Anthony just looked pained. 'And it was one of those new types, with the flat plastic lid that it stands on, so the sauce is always ready to be squeezed out. And I thought to myself, instead of calling it ketchup, they ought to call it ketch-down.'

Stephanie chortled with laughter, thumping a hand on the table, making wine slosh out of her glass. 'Stop! You're killing me. These new jokes are great.'

Max gave a little clap. Anthony just smiled.

Edith winced. 'It was the delivery, wasn't it? Not snappy enough? Too long to get to the punchline.'

'It's not that….' Max began.

'It was great,' Anthony said. 'Really. Do you have … any others?'

'I'm rubbish, aren't I?' Edith said. 'Just admit it.'

'It's only a village festival,' Anthony said. 'They're not expecting Jasper Carrott.'

'I'll get dragged off stage,' Edith said.

'Put in the Wicker Man,' Max added.

Stephanie burst into laughter again. 'Shut up! It was great! Tell the one about the rabbit that eats fingers again. Go on!'

'I'm saving that for the festival,' Edith said. 'If nothing else, it'll kill a bit of time.'

'Honestly, it's not that bad,' Anthony said. 'You have some good jokes.'

'Some?'

'I didn't really get the one about sparrows, but the others were … interesting.'

'Look, just put me out of my misery.' Edith picked up her glass of wine. 'Anyway, time for the main event. Stephanie, you're up.'

Stephanie's expression of delight turned to one of horror. 'Me?'

'Yes, you promised. Unlike me, you have an actual talent.'

'I can't.'

'Please? Just one song.'

Stephanie took a deep breath. Max smiled and reached out a hand, taking hers. Stephanie nodded. 'Only one song.'

They carried their wine through to the room with the piano. Stephanie swallowed the rest of her glass in one gulp, then pulled out the stool and sat down. Max put his hands on her shoulders. Edith felt a pang of jealousy and inched a little closer to Anthony, but if he got the hint, he showed no sign, standing a polite distance away with his glass of wine in his hands.

'All right,' Stephanie said, and from the tremble in her

voice, Edith knew she was on the verge of tears. She suddenly felt horrible for forcing this on Stephanie, and stepped forwards, about to tell her friend to stop, when Stephanie's hands fell on the piano keys, and the first delicate chord rang out.

It was like a floodgate had opened. At first Stephanie's hands moved slowly, working their way up and down the keys, then as her confidence grew, she began to play faster and with more fluidity, feet working the pedals, head swaying back and forth as the music rose and fell. The minutes passed, Stephanie playing a complex jazz piece that had Edith, Anthony and Max entranced. Then, just as her fingers started to slow, she played a rapid rock chord and the song turned into Elton John's *Crocodile Rock*.

'Here we go!' Max shouted. Anthony added a 'Whoop!' and Edith began to clap. They didn't really know the words, but with Stephanie taking the lead, they were all soon bellowing along.

With the others laughing as Stephanie played the last chord, she turned and said, 'And this one's by Billy Joel.'

After a raucous *Piano Man*, Stephanie started to take requests. Even with songs she didn't know, if it was famous enough, she had enough skill to pull off a decent rendition. By the time she pushed back the stool and said her hands were aching, it was nearly ten o'clock.

'We'd better get back,' Anthony said.

Edith glanced at Stephanie, who shrugged. 'You can stay here if you like,' she said. 'I mean, there are tons of empty rooms. I'm sure we could find you something without too many cobwebs.'

'It wouldn't be gentlemanly,' Anthony said, in a way that had Edith, a couple of glasses of wine past her usual limit, squirming. 'And I wouldn't want Pickles to find out.

Don't worry, we have a cabin at the timber merchant that Granddad keeps ready in case we have a late job.'

'Or a staff party,' Max said. 'Plus, I've heard this place is haunted. No offence, but I'll take a cabin in the woods over a haunted mansion.'

'In that case we'll walk you back,' Stephanie said.

Max and Anthony exchanged glances. 'You'll walk us back?'

Stephanie shrugged. 'It's a modern world.'

Max squeezed her hand. 'No one would mess with you, my love.'

Edith wanted to be sick, while at the same time wishing it was Anthony's hand in hers. He stood a little over to the side, and while she glanced at him, he kept his eyes firmly on the ground.

'All right,' Max said. 'How about just to the end of the drive? It's about halfway anyway.'

'Deal,' Stephanie said.

They headed out. It was a cold but chilly November night, the moon nearly full, glowing orange, the stars a tapestry of twinkling lights. Edith, having spotted a couple of shooting stars, looked down to realise Stephanie and Max had quickly forged ahead, their voices soft as they walked close to each other. Feeling a momentary panic, she looked around, then found Anthony's outline close by.

'Are you all right?' he asked.

'Just a little….' Drunk was the word she wanted, but it was somehow inappropriate. 'Overawed,' she said instead. 'Thanks for helping us out. We literally couldn't have done it without you two.'

'Anytime,' he said. They walked on a few more steps. Edith realised she was deliberately walking slowly, almost limping, giving Stephanie and Max time to stretch the distance.

What am I playing at? How drunk am I?

'You know,' Anthony said after an uncomfortable silence, 'I forgive you for pushing me in the school pond.'

'Ah, thanks.'

'I mean, it wasn't the outcome I was hoping for at the time, but it was nice to have some contact with you. I mean, having you shove me in the back was better than being ignored.'

'What … what were you hoping for?'

'Do you remember the game we were playing?'

Edith smiled. Her heart, though, was hammering, making it uncertain whether she would be able to speak clearly. 'Y … yeah. Kiss-chase.'

Anthony just chuckled.

(don't say it; don't say it; don't say it)

'What if I caught you now?'

Her hands were trembling. She realised she had stopped walking, Anthony stopping with her.

'Edith,' he said, moving close to her in the dark. He was little more than a shadow looming over her. 'I think you're lovely. I mean, your jokes, they're something else, but you're just so kind and nice, and you're beautiful.'

Will you catch me if my legs give way?

His hand had slipped into hers. Another slid around her waist, gently, just tight enough to keep her steady.

'Are there any ponds near here?' she whispered, voice shaking.

'I hope not.'

She could smell him now, the musky scent of man, mingled with a little wine. She squeezed his hand tight as though to tell him it was okay.

His lips lightly brushed hers. Edith wondered if she was going to die. She held onto him, wondering how far he would go, but he kept it light, respectful. When he pulled away, she found herself gasping for air.

'Lunch in the pub tomorrow?' he whispered, and somehow the night air and the chill made his words sound romantic.

'I'll be there at twelve,' Edith said.

'Do you want me to pick you up and we can walk down together?'

'It's okay. I have to go to the shop, talk to Barbara about a couple of things.'

'Sure.'

Anthony squeezed her hand again, and this time drew her into his chest, hugging her tightly. He was strong: she could feel the muscles through his jumper. Powerful from hauling wood for a living yet gentle, as though he could cradle an injured bird in his hands.

'Did you get lost?' came Max's shout back down the path, followed by a snort of laughter from Stephanie. 'Do you want to borrow a map?'

'We'd better hurry up,' Anthony said, but as he turned, Edith slipped her hand into his, and they walked hand in hand the rest of the way out to where the others waited.

22

A SPANNER IN THE WORKS

'Coffee,' Stephanie said, sliding a mug across the table to Edith as she stumbled into the kitchen, eyes sore, hair feeling like an explosion, head shuddering.

'How much did I drink?'

'Hardly anything. You're such a lightweight.'

'I feel like I drank the entire cellar.'

'No, some of it's still there. I checked. So, Anthony?'

Edith felt her cheeks flush. 'I think I got a little carried away.'

Stephanie beamed. 'Wouldn't you just tell me to go with it?'

'Yeah, probably. It was just a … thing, though. I mean, he might have forgotten about it by this morning.'

'I doubt it.'

'He was probably just drunk.'

'I only saw him have one glass of wine. Max said he hardly drinks.'

'He won't have much interest in a lush like me, then.'

'You're not a lush. You're just a lightweight.'

Wanting to change the subject, Edith said, 'So, are you going to play at the festival this weekend?'

Stephanie's smile dropped. 'It's one thing playing for some friends. Totally another playing in front of a crowd.'

'Yet you're quite happy to watch me humiliate myself?'

'You kind of volunteered. Plus, your jokes are pretty good.'

'You're the only one who laughed.'

'Just wait until Saturday I bet loads of people will laugh. But seriously, I know what you're trying to do, but I just don't think I can.'

'A few days ago, you wouldn't play in front of anyone at all.'

Stephanie shrugged. 'I think I'd had a glass of wine or two too many myself. I don't think I could do it again.'

'Please? I'm scared.'

Stephanie looked down at her hands, cradling a mug of coffee. She lifted it to her lips and finished it in a single swallow.

'I think we'd better get back to work,' she said. 'We've been slacking off a lot lately, haven't we?'

Without waiting for a reply, she got up and headed out of the kitchen.

~

The morning passed in a hungover blur. The best way to deal with it was to throw herself into cleaning, Edith found, so she grabbed a cloth and a bucket and wiped surfaces until her hands were chapped and sore. The hours ticked by. Only when an old juddery grandfather clock chimed twelve did she remember her date with Anthony. She jumped up and ran down to the kitchen, where Stephanie was packing sandwiches into a hamper.

'Oh, sorry, I forgot to tell you that I'm meeting Max for a lunchtime picnic. I'll be back by two o'clock.'

Edith smiled. 'I'm meeting Anthony for lunch in the pub.'

Stephanie let out a whoop. 'Look at us. Do you need some paracetamol?'

'Maybe just one. Just in case.'

They said their goodbyes, Stephanie heading up to the timber merchant, while Edith went downhill into Trenton. The village looked lovely, the autumn leaves fluttering around her as she walked briskly down the hill, worried about keeping Anthony waiting. There was no time to go to the shop before half past twelve, so she headed straight for the pub. To her surprise, there were several cars in the pub car park, and most of the outdoor tables were occupied. As she went inside and saw Matt standing behind the bar, she gave him a shrug of surprise.

'What's with all the business?' she asked. 'Isn't it Wednesday?'

Matt gave her a sheepish grin. 'Festival business,' he said. 'People have started showing up early this year. The guesthouse up the road is full, apparently.'

'Why? I thought you said it was a pretty small event.'

'Don't worry, it is. You'll be fine.'

'Excuse me?'

Edith looked up as a couple of middle-aged ladies approached the bar. Both looked a little nervous. One had a bead of sweat running down the side of her face as though she had been running.

The second nudged the first aside as though eager to speak. 'I'm a huge fan of your work,' she said. 'I've seen everything you've written.'

'Ah—'

'We can't wait to hear you speak on Saturday,' the other said. 'I don't suppose you could sign this flyer?'

She held out a copy of the festival flyer. Edith stared at it, then looked up at Matt.

'This isn't the same one you gave me.' She pointed at the words '*Hollywood's Ellen Davies in conversation*' printed along one side.

Matt shrugged, then gave her an apologetic smile. 'Second printing, I'm afraid. A bit of a mix-up with names. Not that many people good with spelling around here.'

'*Transcendent* was the best show I've seen this year,' the first woman said.

'I'm afraid there's been a little misunderstanding,' Edith said, glaring at Matt and then turning to the two old ladies. 'I'm Edith, Ellen's sister.'

'Oh, you look so much alike. Is she here? Can we meet her?'

'I don't know where she is,' Edith said.

'That's a shame. Will she be doing a meet and greet after the show on Saturday? We're so excited.'

Edith could only stare open-mouthed. 'Coffee please,' she muttered to Matt, then gave the two ladies another awkward smile as they shuffled back to their table. A couple of others sitting nearby started to rise, only for one of the first pair to say, 'It's okay; that's not her; that's just her sister.'

Just her sister. Like a knife jabbing into Edith's back.

'Have you seen, Anthony?' she said to Matt, struggling to find any enthusiasm for her upcoming date. All she wanted to do right now was go home—to her old flat in Brentwell—and bury her head under her blankets. But she couldn't even do that, and second best—her parents' place, was also out of bounds, taken over by James Archer-Pickles.

Who was she? Nobody. Her sister's pale shadow. A part-time homeless cleaner.

As she took her coffee, brushed off another apology from Matt, and then went to a corner table, she could only hope that Anthony might show up soon to make her feel better.

Twelve-thirty came and went. So did one o'clock. At one-fifteen Edith took out her phone to give him a call, but she had neither taken his number nor had any reception. Instead, painfully aware she had been stood up, she ordered another coffee and a sandwich from a continually apologising Matt, even as other customers came into the bar, glanced at her, then engaged each other in quiet—but not quiet enough—conversations.

'She looks a lot like Ellen, doesn't she?'

'You can tell they're sisters.'

'They're so similar, but she's not quite as glossy.'

At one-thirty, Edith, by now spitting bricks and with fire shooting out of her ears, aggressively paid Matt then headed back up the hill towards the house. Buzzing from too much coffee but fuming with anger at the festival mix-up, the endless comparisons to her more beautiful and more successful sister, and the fact that Anthony had stood her up, she felt almost witchlike powers as she summoned a sudden thundercloud to appear out of nowhere and open its gates just as she reached a section of the hill without any tree cover.

In moments she was soaked. Giving up even trying to get dry, she looked up at the sky as the rain hammered her face and screamed, 'Leave me alone, you stupid rain! Can't you see my life is rubbish enough already?'

The growl of a car engine made her turn. James Archer-Pickles's Porsche came gliding slowly up the road behind her.

Ellen stepped onto the verge as it came up alongside and the passenger window slid down.

'Can I offer you a ride?' James said, perfectly smug and manicured from inside the warm, dry interior. 'Not the best of days to be out and about, is it?'

Edith wanted nothing more than to tell him to get lost, but she was cold, soaked and miserable. She nodded and went to open the door.

'Hang on,' James said, reaching into the back seat. He pulled an old blanket from somewhere and laid it across the passenger seat. 'Sorry, it's a rental. I can't have you getting the upholstery wet. Luckily, I keep this old dog blanket with me in case I pick anyone up.'

Edith, who already felt like a fence post banged halfway into the ground, felt another humiliating clunk on her overworked head. As she sank a couple more inches into the ground, she gave a slow nod.

'Okay,' she said.

'Right, in you get,' James said.

Edith opened the door and climbed in on top of the grey blanket, dog hairs immediately sticking to her jeans. She pulled the door shut and James started the car moving forwards again.

'What happened to you?' he said. 'You look terrible. I don't mean your looks—you're a solid eight out of ten on a good day—but in general. Did someone dunk you in the river?'

'Life did.'

'Ah, that's too bad. Perhaps you should let me take you out on that date you keep stubbornly resisting. Behind the smooth, wealthy exterior, I'm just a guy like all the others.'

'I'll think about it.'

'So, what happened?'

Edith wasn't sure which of her problems to choose.

Not quite low enough yet to succumb to his slimy charm, she said, 'I got stood up.'

'Oh? What idiot would do that to you?'

She thought she might as well go all in. 'Anthony Wallen. He works at the timber merchant.'

James burst out laughing. 'That meathead who showed up at my—sorry, your—house the other day? Seriously? And you turned me down? I know women like a bit of rough, but that's like dating sandpaper. Come on, Ellen—sorry, that's a joke—you can do better than a country bumpkin like that. Five kids and a council house? Sitting at home watching *Eastenders* while he goes down the pub and talks about football and power saws with his spongy-brained mates? Great life you'll have there.'

'I like him,' Edith muttered.

'I went to Cannes last year,' James said. 'And Grandfather has a yacht in Monaco. Ever been there? How about I take you there for our first date? It'll be your sister wishing she was you once you're hanging off my arm.'

Edith just stared straight ahead. The huge, expensive wipers slid back and forth across the windscreen, swiping the rain away as though trying to erase nature itself. She slumped back in the seat, leaning her face into the smelly dog blanket, and was about to close her eyes when she saw a figure moving through the rain up ahead.

Anthony.

Edith jerked upright. He was jogging along the road, one hand over his head to ward off some of the rain.

'Huh, well look who it is,' James said.

'Can he see us?'

'No, tinted windows. Keeps out the paupers.' James chuckled. 'Let's give him a taste of what he's missing, though.'

'No, don't—'

As Anthony came alongside, James wound down the passenger side window. Edith squirmed in the seat as Anthony paused to look in, his mouth falling open.

'You snooze, you lose,' James sneered, then wound the window up before Anthony could say anything. Edith sat up, reaching for the door handle, but James hit the accelerator and the car jumped forwards. In the rearview mirror she watched Anthony fade from sight.

'Stop! Let me out!' Edith scrambled for her phone as James sped up, bumping along the uneven lane. 'I'll call the police!'

'Relax, I'm just taking you back to the house. Sorry, I couldn't resist taunting that clown.'

'Stop the car right now!'

'Sure, as you wish.' James touched the brakes and the car came to a gentle stop. Edith peered out into the rain and saw they had arrived at the gates to Trenton Manor. 'Do you need an umbrella?' James asked.

'No, I'll be fine.'

'You can take that blanket if you like,' James said.

'Thanks for the lift,' she snapped, then opened the door and climbed out.

'I'll be round with your pay envelopes tomorrow,' James said. 'Don't forget, the offer's still open. Cannes, Monaco, anywhere you want. I'll treat you like a princess.'

Edith said nothing. Mustering the last of her strength, she slammed the car door shut, turned and stalked up the driveway as the rain hammered down around her.

23

MISDIRECTION

'Oh dear, did you get caught out in it?' Stephanie said, standing in the entrance as a soaked Edith stumbled into the porch. 'I only just got back in time. Didn't you take an umbrella?'

Edith shook her arms, water dribbling onto the stone floor. 'Clearly not,' she said.

'Well, good news. Max gave me a big box of cocoa which Rick said fell off the back of a lorry.'

'Ah, you probably shouldn't have accepted that—'

'Literally off the back of a lorry. His friend is a delivery driver, and sometimes things get knocked over. He got rear-ended by a tractor at a junction and ended up with five boxes of hot chocolate he couldn't deliver.'

At the thought of a steaming cup of hot chocolate, Edith's frustrations melted away. 'I don't suppose you have marshmallows we can put in it?'

Stephanie grinned. 'Of course. Chocolate sprinkles, cinnamon sugar, and a box of flakes.'

'I need to comfort eat. Right now.'

'Technically it's a drink.'

'Well, you make the hot chocolate while I eat the flakes. Whatever's left we'll put in the drink.'

'Deal. Don't worry, I've eaten six already.'

They went through into the kitchen. Stephanie made the hot chocolate, and Edith's frustrations gradually began to deflate. Stephanie nodded along as Edith gradually relayed what had happened.

'You need to go and see Anthony,' Stephanie said. 'I don't know why he stood you up, but you need to go and see him. Isn't that what you would have said to me?'

Edith sighed and nodded. 'Yeah, but it's so much easier to tell someone else to do it than to do it yourself.'

'Tell me about it.'

'So … how are you and Max?'

Stephanie's face paled. 'He threw me in at the deep end. He knew I was nervous about meeting his mother, so he had her show up at the picnic we had down by Willow River. I was mortified, but she was actually really nice. She wants to take me shopping next week sometime. Oh, and do you think we'll be finished up here pretty soon? Max's family have a villa in the south of France which they always go to over Christmas.' Stephanie smiled and let out a long, contented sigh. 'There's a Christmas market, and carol singers, and he said it's just idyllic.'

Edith couldn't help but feel a pang of jealousy. On the one hand, she was glad everything was working out for her friend, but on the other, she wished a little of Stephanie's luck would fall her way. Mind you, a millionaire playboy wanted to take her to Cannes. Perhaps she ought to take James up on his offer after all; perhaps beneath the obnoxious, spoiled and unpleasant exterior, there was a semblance of a decent human being.

'It sounds lovely,' she said. 'I'm pleased for you, really I am.'

Autumn on Maple Tree Lane

'Maybe you and Anthony could come along—'

Edith put up a hand. 'I don't think so.'

'Are you going to go and see him?'

'Yeah, maybe, in a bit.'

It was easily to get back into her work. Later in the afternoon, Roger called back to say he had spoken to Lawrence, who knew a Latin scholar. If they were in tomorrow, the man was willing to stop by in the morning and take a look at the document. Even though her enthusiasm had dimmed somewhat, Edith agreed. It probably was just an ancient bank statement, but at least it was a mystery they could put to rest.

'By four o'clock, the thunderclouds were long gone, and an aquamarine sky hung overhead. Chilly winds rustled the trees. Reluctant, Edith stood by the front door, looking out.

'It's cold,' she said.

'Go on, you need to go and speak to him,' Stephanie urged her, not quite physically barring her from coming back inside, but close enough to suggest that the option existed. With the daylight fading, Edith only had half an hour or so to get over to the timber merchant before she'd be walking back in the dark. With a concealed scowl at Stephanie, she stepped out into the cold.

As she walked up the driveway and turned onto Maple Tree Lane, she pondered what she would say to Anthony when she saw him. She felt like one of those cartoon characters with an angel sitting on one shoulder and a devil on the other. The angel was telling her that Anthony was a kind and decent human being, despite his lowly status in life, and that she should hold their treasured moonlit kiss dear, and apologise while letting him explain what had made him late. The devil, on the other hand, was telling her that James was right, that no relationship with

Anthony would ever amount to much, unless her ideal way to spend a Saturday was pushing a pram of screaming children around Tesco while hunting for the best bargains on the reduced counter, while Anthony was out spending most of his meagre salary in the bookies instead of fixing their leaking roof.

Something like that.

By the time she reached the turning into the timber merchant, with the chill starting to encroach on her personal space like an old school bully just released from prison, the devil was winning. She walked up the lane in the semi-darkness, pausing only briefly to pat a disgruntled Marge on the head as the old dog trotted out to give her a gruff bark.

Lights were on in the cabin at the back of the timber merchant. Edith took a deep breath and walked up to the door, lifting a hand to knock on the cold frosted glass. A shadow moved behind it, then the door swung open.

'Sorry to just show up, like this, but I wanted to tell you that I don't think—'

Rick lifted an eyebrow. 'Oh, hello, lass. You're after Anthony, I suppose? I'm afraid the boys have gone already.' He grinned. 'Gone down the pub to watch the football, I imagine.'

Edith's worse fears were already coming true. Rugby, she could accept. But football … images of a future chained to a kitchen sink swirled in her mind, pasty-faced children with claws and teeth ripping at her ankles, leaving them bloody and raw. And there, in the corner, a television playing one of her sister's newest hit series, while above it, a framed picture of a glossy, attractive young woman, next to a pale imitation, prematurely grey, leaning on a stick, face lined and blotchy like a t-shirt dropped behind the washing machine after a wash and left there for years and years and years—

'Lass, if you scream like that for much longer you're going to start attracting the owls.'

Edith blinked. 'Huh?'

'You were wailing like some kind of old washerwoman who's dropped her last powder in the ditch on the way down the river. You know what I'm saying?'

Edith shook her head. 'No. Not really. I think I'm having a breakdown.'

'Why don't you come in and have a cup of tea?'

Edith gave a dumb nod. Rick stepped back to allow her to enter the cabin, and she practically fell over the step into the warm interior.

'I'll put the kettle on. You sit down on that bench there, maybe have a flick through one of those garden shed magazines to calm yourself down a bit.

Edith stumbled down the cabin to a wooden bench and plonked herself heavily down on a threadbare seat cushion. The magazines lying on the tabletop were literally about garden sheds, as well as fencing solutions, decking, and all manner of other wood and DIY based projects. Edith flicked through a couple, an uneasy sense of calm coming over her.

Rick brought her a cup of tea. 'That'll sort you out,' he said. 'Need any more sugar, let me know.'

Edith lifted the cup and took a sip, nearly spitting it back out. 'How many did you put in?'

'Three, heaped. Best thing for a bit of stress. Got to get your sugar levels up.'

'Uh, thanks.'

'I'll give the lad a call in a bit, see if he can come and pick you up.'

'Anthony? Won't he be down the pub watching the football?'

'Ha, no, just messing with you. His mum's got a bit of a cold, so he nipped out early to pick up something for dinner. She's a frail one, my Lisa. Never liked the cooler weather.'

'He's looking after his mother?'

'Yes. He's a good lad. Couldn't wish for a better grandson. Strong as an ox, kind as a fairy godmother, ha. Lets women walk all over him, to be honest. You'd better not be planning on doing that, lass.'

'I—'

'Boy was moping about all afternoon. No idea what got into him. Nearly had to give him a paddle on the backside with my spade, wake him up a bit.'

'He … ah, didn't say?'

'Only that he'd missed his date with you. Didn't give him an earful, did you? He had to run my Lisa into the docs to get her prescription, and there was an accident up on the Brentwell road.'

'An accident?'

Rick grinned. 'You gave him a right earful, didn't you?'

'No, I didn't even see him.'

'Ah well, probably just had Matt give him a piece of his mind about standing up a pretty girl.'

Edith took a sip of the sugar with a dash of tea and grimaced. 'Um, maybe.'

'So, do you want me to give him a call?'

'No, it's okay. Maybe I'll stop by tomorrow. Anyway, thanks for the tea. I'd better get back before it gets too dark.'

Rick grinned. 'And the wolves be running.'

'Um, yeah.'

'Don't worry, Marge'll scare them off.'

24

CONFRONTATION

'Right, that's the last of the boxes from the second floor,' Stephanie said, dropping down a cardboard box overflowing with old fishing magazines, their corners curled and brittle, the pictures on the front of middle-aged men holding up oversized trout dusty and faded. 'At least when your playboy shows up, he can see how much we've done.'

The tinkling of the doorbell made them both turn.

'Talk of the devil—'

'Good morning!' James said, marching through the door without being asked. He looked freshly manicured in a crisp suit and tie, his shirt alone probably costing more than all Edith's worldly possessions. His hair was gelled and slick, and he smelled faintly of cologne. He slipped a hand inside his jacket and pulled out two brown envelopes that looked previously used. 'Here's what you've both been waiting for. But … I'd like to take a quick inspection, if you don't mind. Just to make sure you've earned your money.'

Edith and Stephanie shared a glance. 'Sure,' Edith said. 'Would you like to start with the downstairs toilets?'

James chuckled. 'Really stepping out of your sister's shadow, aren't you?'

'It wasn't a joke.'

'Let's hope those toilets aren't, either.'

With the build and size of a WWE female wrestler, Edith was half hoping Stephanie might throw him through a window or at least put him into a headlock until he had learned some manners, but Stephanie just stepped back to let Edith take the lead.

'This way,' she said through gritted teeth.

James, humming brightly to himself, followed them from room to room as they gave him a muted tour. From time to time he muttered something like, 'We'll have this as the pool room,' or 'This would look much improved with a casino table.'

Finally as they descended from the first floor back to the entrance, Edith turned to him and said in a terse voice, 'Did everything meet your expectations?'

'More or less,' James said. 'In fact, you've done a great job. I've decided to give you a pay rise. How does an extra forty pence an hour sound? It adds up, you know. Over a week that's about five pounds extra, almost half a pint in that ridiculously overpriced pub down the road there.'

'*You're* giving us a pay rise?' Edith said.

James lifted an eyebrow. 'Oh, did I forget to mention it? Grandfather died in the night. I know, heartbreaking. That means that within a few days, this whole sorry heap will belong to me, and since you were working for my grandfather, that means you'll technically be working for me.' He lifted a finger. 'I'm talking about next week, by the way. This week you're on the same rate you started on.'

Edith couldn't bring herself to speak, but Stephanie frowned. 'Aren't you … sad?'

James shrugged. 'I barely knew the man. He patted me

on the head from time to time, and allegedly paid for my private education at Harrow. Oh, and I used to get a Harrods gift voucher for five hundred pounds every birthday and Christmas. Such a skinflint. You can't get anything decent for under a thousand there.'

Edith glared at Stephanie, willing her to be quiet, but Stephanie was shaking her head.

'I never knew my grandfather,' she said. 'But my dad left me. There hasn't been a day since when I haven't wished he was here beside me.'

'You need to get yourself a decent car,' James said. 'It'll put your family right out of your mind. Right, well, I'll leave you to it. And you, Ellen—sorry, Edith—don't forget to give me a call if you change your mind about that hot date. Seriously, helicopter to Cannes tickle your fancy? It can be arranged.'

Edith started to shake her head, but through the open door she saw a figure approaching up the driveway, and her breath caught.

Anthony.

She had wanted to go and see him again, but hadn't known what to say. Perhaps it was better just to let it go, to put it all to bed. She started to shrink back away from the door, but he was too fast, jogging up to the doorway and lifting his hand to knock even as James pulled it open.

'Good morning,' Anthony said with a bright smile, one that dropped at the sight of James. 'Oh. I saw your car. I thought you might have broken down. It's looking a bit scuffed along the sides there. Must be a nightmare with all the brambles around here.'

'Sorry, did someone order some trees to be chopped down?' James said. He looked around at Edith and Stephanie. 'Either of you? No?' He turned back to

Anthony. 'Then what are you doing here on private property?'

'I—'

'Here to clean the drains? You're not really dressed for it, are you? Or is it pest control?'

Anthony's face hardened. Edith tensed, afraid Anthony might give James the haymaker to the jaw that he so definitely deserved, but Anthony just took a step back and crossed his arms over his chest.

'I came to see the girls,' he said. 'It's a private matter.'

'Look how excited they are to see you,' James said. Then, with a scowl that seemed aimed at all of them at once, he went out through the door and strode off up the driveway.

'Well, that was nice,' Anthony said, giving Edith an apologetic smile that immediately broke her heart. She felt tears spring to her eyes and she looked around for Stephanie, wanting moral support, but Stephanie was melting away down the hall, and gave her a brief thumbs up before disappearing down the stairs to the kitchen.

'Hi,' Edith said. 'Don't mind him. He's a total pig.'

'I noticed. Where does he get off speaking to people like that?'

'It comes from being totally loaded I suppose.'

'My grandfather is totally loaded and he's not like that. I think he's just a bit of a clown.' He smiled. 'Look, I'm sorry about yesterday. I—'

'Your grandfather explained. I wasn't mad at you, I just … you know … it was raining, and … he just came driving past and I was already soaked, and—'

Anthony seemed to float across the hall and take her in his arms. Edith found herself crying as she pressed her face into his chest. 'It was all so stupid. I was going to come and see you after James had gone—'

'Well, I had to come up here anyway. Two birds with one stone and all that.'

Edith pulled away. 'What do you mean?'

Anthony smiled. 'I got a call from a mate to say someone at Trenton Manor needed some Latin translated. I thought that meant yourself and Stephanie.'

'Latin? You?'

Anthony shrugged. 'I have a PhD in classical literature from Oxford University.' He grinned. 'Not just a lumberjack, you know.'

'I don't ... why didn't you say?'

'You didn't ask. Look, labels and statuses don't bother me. I don't like people that throw them around, so I don't throw mine around.'

'Your status?'

'I've written a couple of books, that's all. Translating classics. I sometimes get asked to do keynote speeches at foreign universities, that kind of thing. It's fun, but its intermittent. The timber merchant has been in my family for years so I help out whenever I can. Plus, carrying all that wood makes you strong, and being outside a lot keeps you healthy.'

'But ... you get to speak at universities?'

'I was in Istanbul last month, Stockholm three months ago. I have to turn down some requests due to logistics, and quite often I have to pay my own travel expenses.'

'That's still amazing.'

'It is what it is. I told you, I don't care about that kind of stuff, so I don't use it to define me.'

'I thought you just carried wood about for a living.'

'Most of the time I do. Did that bother you?'

Edith wrapped her hands around his waist. She wanted to squeeze him until they were permanently fused. 'I worried that it would, but it didn't. Not one bit.'

'I'm never going to own a Porsche.'

'The only people I've met who own Porsches have been total clowns.'

'How many have you met?'

Edith lifted a finger. 'Just one.' She was about to say something more when she heard footsteps on the gravel outside. She leaned past Anthony to see an irate-looking James come jogging back up the driveway.

'Oh, how cosy,' James snapped. 'Did either of you see where my car keys got to? I think I must have dropped them somewhere around here.'

Edith opened her mouth to speak, but Stephanie's voice came from behind her, and she looked around to see her friend looming in the corridor with a thin smile on her face.

'I know,' she said. 'You dropped them on the gravel outside. I was going to pick them up for you, but a hawk got there first. I think it must have been collecting items to make a nest. It dropped them on a lower branch of a tree just over there.'

They all looked. Something glinted in the sunlight about eight feet off the ground. Edith frowned at Stephanie, who just shrugged, then tucked her hands up under her arms and gave a quick, 'Cluck … cluck.'

'Do you have a ladder?' James snapped.

'There's one in the shed, but it's a bit old,' Edith said. 'You can try it if you like. Or I suppose you could walk up to Wright's Garden Centre on the Brentwell Road. It's only a couple of miles.'

James scowled. 'My car had better be there when I get back.'

'I'm sure it will,' Edith said. 'Unless a tractor comes along and tows it.'

James gave one last scowl, then turned and took off

running up the driveway. Edith waited until he was out of sight, then looked at up Stephanie and Anthony.

'Anyone for coffee?'

Stephanie gave a thumbs up. Anthony nodded, then said, 'Sounds good. After that we'll have a look at that document, shall we?'

25

A THRILLING DISAPPOINTMENT

'It's in here,' Edith said, unable to resist taking Anthony by the hand and leading him through the door. His palm was warm, his fingers calloused but strong. Behind them, Stephanie squeezed into the tiny rooftop room, and together they crowded around the table.

Anthony leaned close, then pulled a torch out of his pocket and shone the light on the glass, illuminating the words beneath.

'Wow, it's pretty old,' he said. 'There, you're right, 1885. How bizarre.'

'Do you know what it says?'

He ran a finger along the glass. 'It's a bit faded, but the handwriting is pretty good. Educated, I suppose you'd say. This was clearly written by someone with a good level of education. Probably someone wealthy, just going on the date. School wasn't mandatory past the age of ten back then, and Latin certainly wasn't. This person was probably privately educated.'

Edith nudged him in the stomach. 'Are you purposely dragging this out? Come on, put us out of our misery.'

Anthony grinned. 'Hang on a sec. I don't want to make any mistakes. Wow, this is crazy. I've never read anything like this before.'

'What ... does ... it ... say?'

Anthony chuckled. 'It's a deathbed confession. "My wish is that my folly be revealed only after I have descended to my grave. My greatest of shames, the one which has been a thundercloud over my head all these many long years. That I lived off my shame is to my regret, despite the joy it brought to my family. That I set another family to ruin and the shame of such is the punishment I bear. It is my only hope that my descendants learn of my folly and one day set to rights what I have done."'

'Wow, do you think he's ever going to get to the point?' Edith said.

'He's certainly taking the scenic route,' Anthony said, following the words with his finger. 'Ah, we're getting to it now. "It is my confession, now, at the moment of my impending death, that I reveal on the night of 31st October 1843, that I, Albert Pickles did engage in a game of cards with Lord Marcus Manfield of Trenton Manor. The lord, rather inebriated, offered, in the presence of three other local men of repute and character, the opportunity to gamble for the ownership of the house and grounds within which I now reside. Lord Mansfield was unaware of my former life as a fairground trickster, and I felt sure he would notice the ace I sleeved, or even if not, reveal, upon my claiming of the spoils, that the game was but a jest. However, one of the men present was a local magistrate, and held Lord Mansfield to his honour. There and then, he signed over Trenton Manor to myself, the lowly proprietor of a canned goods store. The Pickles family became lords of Trenton Manor, and the Mansfield family fell into ruin.'"

Anthony looked up. Edith and Stephanie were staring wide-eyed. 'This is something else,' he said. 'Check out what it says down here.' He ran a finger over the glass near the bottom of the letter. '"My shame is that I have waited to make this confession until the moment of my death. I have ordered it hidden until after my passing, and I hope that my descendants, upon discovering it, will make right of my folly and return Trenton Manor to the descendants of Lord Mansfield." This is my last will and testament, witnessed here by Mrs. Josephine Clemont (housekeeper) and Mrs. Loveday Merricroft (seamstress).'"

'He wanted to give the house back to its rightful owners,' Anthony said. 'I wonder who they are? I bet if you had this document officially checked by a lawyer it would be considered legally binding. That would certainly upset Little Lord Fauntleroy down there.'

'It's unbelievable,' Edith said. 'Like, what a thing to find.'

She was so caught up in the letter that for a moment she forgot about Stephanie. When she turned to her friend, Stephanie was staring open-mouthed at the letter on the table.

'My father's name was Mansfield,' she said, in a voice so quiet it was barely audible.

∽

'My real mother died when I was a child,' Stephanie said. 'I don't remember much about her. My dad remarried, and after he left, it was my stepmother who raised me. I've always called her Mum. She did her best, but when she remarried, I could tell how her attention shifted. I was a teenager by then, and I wasn't really that important anymore.'

'And you don't know where your dad is?' Anthony said.

Stephanie sniffed. 'I have just one postcard that he sent me, more than fifteen years ago. He could be alive, I don't know.'

'I'm no lawyer,' Anthony said, 'but I'm pretty sure that in absentia, that would make you the heir to this property, if this document is considered legally binding. I can't comment on that, either, though. You'd have to consult a lawyer.'

'I don't know any.'

Edith glanced at Anthony. 'I bet you do, don't you?'

He grinned. 'As it happens, I do. My mother is a property lawyer. She's feeling a little under the weather, but she'd love to see something like this. We have to be careful not to damage it. If we take a few good photos and then go and see her, we can see what she says.'

Edith felt a little hot under the collar. 'We?'

'Yeah, why not? You don't mind meeting my mother, do you?'

Edith looked at Stephanie, who gave her a wide, knowing grin.

'Don't be scared,' she whispered, loud enough that Anthony started to laugh. 'It'll be easy. Isn't that what you told me?'

⁓

'Look,' Edith said, giving Stephanie a sheepish grin. 'I'm sorry I drank your thousand-pound brandy. Can you forgive me, or are you going to make me pay it off until the end of time?'

Stephanie just laughed. 'It's not mine.'

'I know not technically, but if there's going to be reparations for all the years that your family was cheated out of your fortune, then surely you could claim it as an offset against the interest?'

'Yeah, maybe. This isn't my house, though, is it?'

'Not yet. But it probably will be, once Anthony's mother has seen that letter.'

'I doubt it.'

'Well, if it is, can you give me a decent cleaning bonus? I did a good job, didn't I? I might not be famous, talented or rich, but if nothing else, I can clean pretty well.'

Stephanie grinned. 'How does forty-five pence an hour sound?'

∼

Anthony's mother was supposed to be looking over the copy of the document Edith and Anthony had cobbled together from a number of photographs, but every few seconds she would look up and give Edith a little grin. As though this amused him no end, Anthony would grin also, leaving Edith feeling not unlike a chicken slowly roasting on a spit.

'Have you put the potatoes on?' she said to Anthony after the fifth or six time, but he just squeezed her hand, and she thought, well, it could be worse. *At least she doesn't seem to hate me.*

Finally, though, Mrs. Wallen looked up, adjusted her glasses over her nose, and adopted a solemn, lawyerly look.

'It's a no-go, I'm afraid,' she said. 'I mean, technically it's a translation, but it wasn't issued by any lawyer that I can see, and at this age, it's long past any statute of limitations. It's fine as a historical document, and something that you could definitely kick up a fuss about, but as something legal … you're out of luck.'

'What do I tell Stephanie?'

'That sadly, she's not going to inherit a manor house estate.'

Edith sighed. 'I think I got her hopes up.'

'There's nothing I can do,' Mrs. Wallen said, shaking her head. Then, suddenly brightening up, she added, 'You will stay for dinner, won't you, dear? Anthony's father will be home soon, and we do love to give everyone he brings home a good grilling.'

'I … ah—'

'She's joking,' Anthony said. 'At least, I hope she is.'

'You should have seen the last one he brought home,' Mrs. Wallen said. 'Mandy, wasn't it? She looked like she'd just jumped out of a tree.'

'She was a hairstylist,' Anthony said.

'Not a very good one, by the look of things.' Mrs. Wallen clasped her hands together and tilted her head. 'So … tell me again how you two first met?'

Edith grimaced. 'I suppose originally it was when I pushed him in the school pond,' she said.

Anthony gave her hand another squeeze. 'And I've been pining after her ever since.'

26

MORE SURPRISES

When Edith pulled back the curtains to reveal the weather for the Trenton Harvest Festival, she couldn't help but feel a little disappointed. The sky was a grey blanket, the air filled with drizzle. The thrill of the last few weeks working at Trenton Manor, her growing friendship with Stephanie, the excitement of a budding relationship with Anthony; it all felt dampened by this cold and grey morning on which she was destined to fall flat.

Whether a dozen people came or a thousand, the thought of standing up in front of them and attempting her fledgling comic routine filled her with dread. Even Anthony struggled to find her jokes funny, and the harder Stephanie laughed, the worse the joke probably was; an inverse quality barometer. That Anthony and Max found Stephanie's amusement more entertaining than the jokes themselves was starkly cutting.

She wandered downstairs, the polished stone floors turning her feet into icy lumps. By the time she reached the kitchen she was hopping from foot to foot, wishing she'd paused long enough to put on a pair of socks.

Stephanie was already there, sipping a large cup of coffee at the trestle table in the middle of the vast room. The kitchen was at least warm, Stephanie having put some kindling into the range.

'There's coffee in the filter,' she asked. 'How are you feeling today?'

Edith filled herself a cup, then returned to the table and sat down. 'I should ask you the same thing. You must be so disappointed.'

Stephanie just smiled. 'Ah, it was wishful thinking. It's kind of nice just to know my family was once rich.'

'It's grossly unfair.'

'It's been unfair for the last hundred and fifty years, so there's no point worrying about it now, is there? Two days ago, I was poor old Stephanie, and I'm still poor old Stephanie. Nothing's changed.'

'You're not poor old Stephanie. You're crazily talented Stephanie who technically should be Lady Stephanie of Trenton Manor. That's something, isn't it? Better than being a homeless and soon-to-be unemployed house cleaner.'

'For someone so good at geeing me up, you're not very good at doing it for yourself,' Stephanie said. 'Do you know what you really are, Edith?'

'What?'

'You're a great friend. And that's more important than anything else. You're awesome. You're the kind of person people want around, and do you know what, you're going to prove it today at the festival by being the best person there.'

'I'm going to be rubbish.'

'No, you won't, because if you are, I'm going down with you.'

'What do you mean?'

Stephanie shrugged. 'If you don't mind, I was thinking of accompanying you on the piano. I called Matt last night, and he said they'd have an electric organ on stage for a couple of other acts. He said I was welcome to use it.'

'You're going to give me a soundtrack? What are you going to play?'

'I have absolutely no idea.' Stephanie looked up at the clock. 'But we have about two hours to figure it out.'

'Looking at the weather, I'm pretty sure the festival will be cancelled anyway.'

Stephanie laughed again. 'The forecast is for unseasonably warm weather from lunchtime onwards. There's no escape from your destiny; you know that, don't you?'

Edith took a deep breath and put out a hand. 'If I go down, you go down with me?'

Stephanie took her hand and shook it. 'Like two lead balloons.'

~

Trenton looked delightful as they walked down the hill into the village. The valley was orange-brown with the last leaves of autumn, and the warm sun beaming out of a clear sky shone off the damp grass of the fields.

The cars parked in lines along the verge stretched halfway up the hill. Edith's heart was fluttering long before they reached the little humpback bridge and saw the pub's packed beer garden. Matt, carrying out a tray of drinks, gave them a wave.

In the field behind the village hall, the festival was already underway. Edith and Stephanie wandered among stalls selling homemade cakes, local vegetables, jams, chutneys, wines, beer, coffee, confectionary, past a competition for the harvest's biggest vegetables, a corn doll competition and a scarecrow display, as well as a dozen or so games and activities, including skittles and a shooting gallery. There was a small helter-skelter slide and a bouncy castle, half a dozen children whooping with excitement.

The stage was set up behind the village hall. A small crowd was watching a group of elderly ladies in traditional dress performing a Hawaiian dance. As the music came to a stop, they gave a final pose to a smattering of applause.

'There's us,' Stephanie said, pointing at a signboard beside the stage. 'Well, you, but I did promise.'

Where it said ELLEN DAVIES – TALES FROM HOLLYWOOD, 'Ellen' had been crossed out and 'Edith' written over the top in black marker, while 'Hollywood' had been creatively edited to read 'the woods'.

'They've made it sound like I'm some kind of vagrant,' Edith said.

'At least there won't be so many people here.'

'There she is!'

Edith and Stephanie turned to see a group of middle-aged women come hurrying over. Most of them wore merchandise t-shirts from Ellen's TV show *Transcendent*, some featuring the faces of the main characters, others with the show's logo. Edith could only smile as they gathered round.

'Is it all right to ask for autographs?' one said to Stephanie. 'We promise not to get too close.'

Edith and Stephanie exchanged a glance. 'Look,' Edith said, 'I'd love to sign everything, but, as you can probably see from the sign over there, there's been a late alteration. Ellen Davies can't make it. I'm her less famous, less talented sister.'

'Oh, wow, a family connection!' one said, whistling

through her teeth. 'Can you sign my t-shirt, 'love, Ellen's sister'?' She looked up at Stephanie. 'Is that all right?'

Stephanie could only shrug.

Edith signed a few t-shirts, posters, one forearm, and even the base of a plastic toy, then posed for photos. 'Can I get one with both you and your bodyguard?' one asked. 'Can I pose like I'm about to grab you?'

Edith and Stephanie could only oblige until the group were satisfied. Chattering among themselves, they moved off, leaving Edith and Stephanie alone by the stage.

'So that's what it's like being famous,' Edith said. 'I think I can live without it.'

'Your name's not on the list; you're not coming in,' Stephanie said. Then, with a grin, she added, 'Shall we go and check out Barbara's stall? See how that bread dough we made came out?'

'Good idea.'

The afternoon trickled past, leaving the maximum amount of time possible for Edith's nerves to start jangling. Max and Anthony arrived just as the sun was going down, and a series of portable floodlights came on to illuminate the festival area, but even with Anthony telling her not to worry, Edith was more nerves than person as she waited by the side of the stage, a handful of crumpled notes in her hand. To be fair, the standard of the acts had been pretty low. One local guitarist had had a string break halfway through his first song, and one member of a local troupe of dancing farmers had fallen off the front of the stage. Even so, as she waited for Matt to introduce her, Edith's hands trembled as she looked out over a crowd numbering at least a hundred people.

'Knock them dead,' Anthony said, squeezing her hand. 'And just know that no matter how badly it goes, my mum still thinks you're awesome.'

Edith scowled at him. 'Your support—and your mother's—means so much.'

'Own it,' he said, leaning in and kissing her on the cheek. 'Show them what you've got.'

Matt tapped the microphone. 'Right, everyone, this is our last act of the evening, so don't worry, you can be home in the warm soon. Is anyone else freezing? At least the rain stayed off, eh? Right, so we have a local girl up next. Not the local girl many of you were expecting, perhaps, but you know how it is. Got bums on seats, didn't it?' A murmur of discontent came from the crowd. 'Anyway, to tell you a few jokes I've been assured probably won't upset anyone, and accompanied by Stephanie Madden on piano … Willow River's very own Edith Davies.'

The contingent of Ellen's fans for whom she had done autographs began to cheer, but as Edith climbed up onto the stage, followed by Stephanie, they were met by muted applause. Edith's throat was so tight she could barely speak. She grabbed the microphone, almost dropping it, fumbling for it with hands dripping with cold sweat, clutching it to her chest. She looked out at a couple of hundred faces watching her across a range of emotions, everything from resentment to excitement, and forced a smile.

'Hello,' she said, as Stephanie began to tinkle gently on the electric piano.

A scattering of applause.

'I live up the road,' Edith said. 'Well, I used to. Then my parents threw me out.'

Several people laughed.

'No, no, that's not a joke. That's kind of the truth. Well, they didn't throw me out exactly, but they kind of pushed me out.'

'Put on a bit of weight?' someone shouted as several people laughed. As if in response, Stephanie gave a discordant shriek on the piano.

'Anyway, so I'm homeless now. Except that I'm living in Trenton Manor.'

'One percent homeless!' someone shouted. 'You're all the same!'

'Give us back our public services!' someone else called.

'I'm the cleaner,' Edith said.

'Woo!' someone—possibly Anthony—shouted. Edith glanced down at her crumpled, sweat-stained notes.

'So, I don't know why people call them sparrows,' she said. 'I've never seen them standing in a line.'

A surprising number of people began to laugh. Edith felt a little flutter in her heart, but the shaking in her hands had eased a little. She forced a smile, as though she were in on the joke.

'I was in the supermarket the other day,' she said. 'I bought a bottle of ketchup, one of those types with the flat plastic lid. I don't know why they don't just call it ketch-down.'

Behind her, Stephanie missed a note. Edith glanced back to see her friend's face creased with laughter, tears streaming down her face. In the crowd too, a handful of people seemed vaguely amused, even if the majority still appeared hostile.

Own it.

She glanced down at the side of the stage and saw Anthony standing there. He gave her a brief thumbs-up.

Edith took a deep breath. She pulled the microphone out of the stand and began to stalk up and down the stage, letting the blood run through her veins, allowing her body to loosen up.

'Have you ever had one of those times when you were

in the supermarket, and you bumped into someone you haven't seen for a long, long time, then just as you start a conversation, you see someone else whom you haven't seen for a long, long time, but you like one of those people a little better than the other?'

A few people in the crowd began to nod, a few even to clap.

'So, I was in Tesco the other day, and I bumped into this guy I used to work with. I always had a soft spot for him, with his cute, kind of buck-toothed smile. Well, I was just wondering if it wasn't too late to perhaps get to know each other a little better, when I felt a tap on my shoulder and there was my childhood dentist.'

A few people laughed. One old man in the front row fell off his chair.

'Five minutes later, they left together. My old friend was never the same again.'

With Stephanie seemingly aware of how to play at exactly the right intensity to match Edith's jokes, she began to flow into her routine. Many of her jokes were untested, unfinished even, lacking proper punchlines, but as she felt herself relax, she found the delivery itself getting a laugh out of several jokes only Stephanie had previously found funny.

'It's getting dark,' she said, pointing out behind the crowd at the last glimmer of light behind the hills. 'It's appropriate, I think, because I have one more for you, and it's a little dark.'

'The rabbit one?' Stephanie hissed. Edith glanced back and nodded.

'So, when I was growing up, I had this rabbit,' she said. 'He was a big guy, about the same size as a standard poodle.' Several people laughed. 'His name was Marvin. Now, one day, we found out that he only ate meat.' A few handclaps. 'We started giving him scraps from the table, but my family was pretty poor, and we didn't have much meat to go around. It looked like were going to have to get rid of Marvin. But then one day, I had a friend come round. "He's so cute," he said. "Can I touch him?"' Edith paused looking out at the crowd. Several people were laughing hysterically, and she had a sudden moment of clarity that they were laughing because of something she had said. With a smile, she continued, 'He put his finger in the cage, and Marvin took it straight off.'

Several people cheered. Edith lifted a hand as if to ask for calm. 'Well, anyway, of course he was likely to tell his mum about this, so I told him that Marvin was a clever rabbit, and that he knew how to open the cage, and he could smell blood. That kept my friend quiet.' Edith tapped a finger against the side of her head. 'However, Marvin was still pretty hungry, so I had to make some more friends. Pretty soon, most of the kids in the neighbourhood, at least half of those in my class, they had a finger missing. Yet, afraid of Marvin getting out of his cage and hunting them down, none of them said a thing.'

She paused again, letting Stephanie's music animate her words. 'So, one day, I was walking to school, and I saw this TV station van pulling up outside the school. Curious, I wandered over and asked them what was going on. "We've come to make a documentary," they told me. "You see, there are a lot of kids in this area with only nine fingers. We think there might be something in the water."' Edith paused again, looking out at the crowd, wondering if anyone would get the joke. 'And then one of them noticed me, noticed my two complete hands, and I saw them frowning, wondering what was going on. "It's all right," I told them. "I ... only drink bottled water."' As confused laughter rippled across the crowd, Edith lifted a hand. 'I've been Edith Davies, and on piano was Stephanie Madden. Thank you and good night.'

Cheers—a few of them suitably confused, accompanied them as they climbed down off the stage. Edith's heart was pounding, and Stephanie had tears in her eyes.

'"I only drink bottled water",' she wheezed. 'Oh my God. That's the funniest thing I've ever heard.'

Edith grimaced, catching Anthony's eyes. 'Yet, I'm not sure why. I really need to work on that one.'

'You were awesome,' Anthony said. 'That was just great.'

'Impressive,' came a familiar voice from behind her, followed by a little clap, and Edith snapped her head around.

A young woman stood behind her, roughly Edith's height and build, a summer hat covering her head, sunglasses on her eyes, skin incongruously tanned, clothing a little too posh for Trenton on a cold Saturday in November.

'*Ellen?*'

Her sister smiled. 'Hi, Edith. Someone sent me a message to tell me I was performing at a local harvest festival.' She lifted an eyebrow. 'Sensing a possible lawsuit, I jetted in to check it out.'

'And … what did you think?'

Ellen reached up and took off her sunglasses, tucking them into a ribbon on her hat. Then, with a wide smile, she lifted her arms. 'I've missed you, sister.'

Edith laughed and pulled her sister into a warm hug. 'It's good to have you back home,' she said. 'Even if it's for what, ten minutes?'

'A couple of days,' Ellen said. 'Wow, I had no idea you had such a … talent.'

'Really?'

'Well, I mean, it needs a bit of work, but I was … I'm not sure "impressed" would be the right word, but definitely … intrigued?'

'I survived it,' Edith said. 'That's good enough for me.'

'Oh, that rabbit joke,' Stephanie said, wiping a tear out of her eye.

Edith opened her mouth to reply, but a sudden shout made them all turn. James Archer-Pickles came marching through the crowd, cheeks flushed as though he'd been partaking in the local cider, fists balled, shirt uncharacteristically untucked, mud flecking his expensive trousers.

'You!' he shouted, pointing a finger. 'What did you do?'

His eyes narrowed on Stephanie as he reached their group. Rick had wandered over with Marge, and the little sausage dog gave a threatening growl. Max glanced at Anthony, then muttered, 'the river or the muck spreader?'

James stopped just out of the reach of the two guys. He poked his finger at Stephanie again. 'Who are you? What trickery did you play on Grandfather?'

'Make sense, boy,' Rick said. 'Sounds like you've got a mouth full of dung.'

'You tricked him, didn't you?'

'Excuse me? I only met him once.'

'Ah, but he knew all about you, didn't he? Just listen to this.' With a petulant snap of his hand, he pulled a crumpled sheet of paper out of his pocket. Edith got a glimpse of a header: Last Will and Testament.

'"…and in order to absolve the sin of my great-grandfather Julius Pickles for the deception that he played on the honourable Lord Marcus Mansfield and his family, I leave Trenton Manor and its estate to Stephanie Madden, formerly Mansfield, the last descendant of the Mansfield family."'

James lowered the paper and glared at Stephanie. 'What witchery did you play on Grandfather Arnold?'

Stephanie just shook her head. 'I had no idea. But … that's very nice of him, isn't it? I hope he didn't leave you with nothing.'

James glared at her. 'He left me three houses in London, a ski lodge in Switzerland and his yacht … but I really wanted that old house!'

He stamped his foot, then began to rip the piece of paper into shreds. Marge barked, then made a dart for one of the falling pieces, chewing it in her little mouth. Ellen, taking a couple of steps back, had pulled out a notebook and was furiously scribbling something down. Max glanced at Anthony and suggested they dunk James in the river, but James suddenly recovered himself enough to shout, 'I hope it rains on the walk home!' then turned and ran back through the crowd until he was lost from sight in the gloom.

Ellen wrote something else, then closed her notebook and slipped it into her coat pocket. 'Oh, wow,' she said. 'He was something else. I could make a whole show around him.'

'What just happened there?' Edith said, glancing at Stephanie.

She gave a dazed shake of her head. 'I'm not quite sure,' she said. Then, with a wide grin, she clapped her hands together. 'Anyone for tea and scones?'

27

FUTURE PLANS

EDITH AND ANTHONY STOOD TOGETHER ON THE driveway outside her house, waiting for her parents' imminent return. The leafless trees swayed in the breeze, and a little of the morning's frost still lingered on the ground. Anthony was shifting from foot to foot, his palm so damp with sweat that Edith had to wipe her hand on her jeans.

'What if they don't like me?' he said, a little tremble in his voice.

'I'm more worried about you liking them,' Edith said, as the door opened behind her, and Ellen came out of the house to stand beside them.

'I can't believe that weirdo,' she said. 'He managed to take the lock off my door and it looked like he was sleeping in my bed, yet when he sees me at that festival, he doesn't recognise me. Seriously, that's fame for you.'

'Ah, here they are,' Edith said, as Rufus and Martha's transit van came chugging into view. It pulled up in the drive and the doors flew open.

'Oh my, what's this? A special greeting?' Martha said,

opening her arms wide. 'Both my little girls at once! And ... Ellen, I take it you brought your bodyguard?'

As Martha hugged Edith and Ellen, Anthony gave a nervous smile. 'I work up at the timber merchant,' he said. 'Anthony Wallen.'

'That's the lad who put in the fence behind the magnolia,' Rufus said. 'Did you pop round for an inspection?'

'Ah, no.'

'Anthony's my ... ah, boyfriend,' Edith said, feeling a little of his awkwardness, even as Ellen laughed.

'Nice to meet you ... again,' Anthony said.

'How lovely,' Martha said with a bright smile. 'It sounds like all sorts has been going on since we were away. Honestly, you go to a wellness retreat for just a couple of weeks ... and everything's different. Your dad's decided Fieldy's full name should be Lord Fielder of Willow River.' She rolled her eyes. 'What happened to the guy with the Porsche?'

'Oh, he's gone to Monaco, apparently,' Edith said. 'In a huff.'

'Not before gluing a picture of his face next to mine in one of my photo albums,' Ellen said. 'Total, total weirdo.'

'Did you finish cleaning the House on Hell Hill?' Rufus asked Edith. 'I suppose you must have done. Where's Stephanie?'

'Ah ... Lady Stephanie of Trenton Manor has gone to Argentina in search of her father.'

'And she's taken Max from the timber merchant,' Anthony said. 'So if you know anyone needing a job, please let us know.'

'Lady ... lumber ... it sounds like we all need a cup of tea.'

'I got a job,' Edith said with a smile. 'I'm now the

manager of the soon-to-open Trenton Manor Wellness Resort. Stephanie … Lady Stephanie asked me to inquire whether you and Mum would be willing to put on a few classes for our guests. Wellbeing type stuff, you know, although you might need to leave Fieldy—I mean, Lord Fielder—at the um, gate. We won't start taking bookings until the new year, but the website's only been live for a few days and she's had several inquiries already.'

'How lovely. Lady Stephanie, doesn't that have a nice ring to it?'

'She said she'd be interested in buying those … displays in the cellar, if you can't find a buyer. Apparently she wants to donate a few things to the National Trust.'

'Oh, how exciting. Well, I'll have to talk to my contacts, now that we're back on the grid. It's so nice to hear you've finally got a proper job, though, dear."

'At least one,' Ellen said. 'I'm trying to get a few dates together for her debut tour on the comedy circuit.'

'Comedy?'

'We're still thinking about that,' Edith said, looking up at Anthony and squeezing his hand. 'We've got Christmas to think about first.'

Martha smiled. 'It sounds like it could be the best one in a while,' she said, looking from one face to another. 'Now, who's for a cup of herbal tea?'

END

ACKNOWLEDGMENTS

Many thanks as always go to those who helped with this book. Jenny for her incredible knowledge and eye for detail, Elizabeth for the cover, and Becky for proofreading. And as always, to my muses, Jenny Twist and John Dalton.

Finally, for those of you who support me via Patreon, thanks very much. In no special order: Donna Askins, Mike Wright, Rosemary Kenny, Jane Ornelas, Ron, Gail Beth Le Vine, Sharon Kenneson, Jennie Brown, Leigh McEwan, Janet Hodgson, and Katherine Crispin.

And for everyone who's Bought me a Coffee recently: Joeann Davis, Allen from the US, Donna Askins, Vicky B, Sherie Williams Ellen, Hairbender, Randall Balsmeyer, Peter Jaspers-Fayer, Sam Cleeve, Cazuma, Patsy Mcclure, Brinda, GreyCynic, Monica Demmerle, Amy Thay, Cesar Sandoval, Ann Chesterton, Nova Kay, Someone, Jennie B, Mary, Richard Herndon, Claire, Ian Yates-Laughton, Jim Naughton, Rowan Anderson, Andrea Richards, Malcolm from Canada, Elizabeth M. Dykes, Rachel G, Keith Turner, Sheri Bellefeuille, Niall Nicolson, Amelie Eva, Paul M, Laurie Jones, Aileen MacKinnon, Att, Irena, Michael

Fidler, Lindsay G Cowan, Spyke, Rosemary, Marianne, Denise Nicholson, Janet, Christine Henderson, Sonia Finch, Matt Korbich, Venita Garnett, Paula Yovanee, Sarah House, Anne, Norma, and Theresa. Thank you. Your support means so much.

Last and not least, to all my readers. Thank you for supporting my books and I look forward to bringing you the next book!

CPW

August, 2024

ABOUT THE AUTHOR

CP Ward is a pen name of Chris Ward, the author of the dystopian *Tube Riders* series, the horror/science fiction *Tales of Crow* series, and the *Endinfinium* YA fantasy series, as well as numerous other well-received stand alone novels. In addition, he writes the critically acclaimed *Slim Hardy Mysteries* under the name of Jack Benton.

Autumn on Maple Tree Lane is the fifth book in the Warm Days of Autumn series.

Expect more soon …

Chris would love to hear from you:
www.amillionmilesfromanywhere.com
chrisward@amillionmilesfromanywhere.net

Printed in Great Britain
by Amazon